MAMMOTH ISLAND

RUSSELL JAMES

SEVERED PRESS
HOBART TASMANIA

MAMMOTH ISLAND

Copyright © 2021 Russell James

WWW.SEVEREDPRESS.COM

ISBN: 978-1-922551-93-1

Other books by Russell James

Dedication

For Janet and all who love the majestic creatures we call elephants.
You are not going to like this story.

CHAPTER ONE

"Now be quiet," Nick said. "We don't want to attract any of the adults."

Kai Nishikawa sure as hell didn't want to do that. Capturing a juvenile was scary enough.

He crouched down beside Nick and two other trappers. Dense bushes obscured them from anything that might wander through the clearing in front of them. Soaring pines surrounded the clearing, and overhead a hazy sky diffused the high Arctic summer sun. Kai smelled pine, peat, and his own nervous sweat.

"Are you sure this is a good idea?" Kai said.

"Popov is ready to bring in the investors," Nick said. "No one is going to buy something they haven't seen."

"This plan seems dangerous."

"You're the one who asked to get out from behind your little accountant's desk and venture into the forest. You can't join us trappers out here and not expect there to be danger. These woods aren't full of Bambi and Thumper."

Nick had that right. Kai had suspected as much when he'd been recruited to manage the books and logistics for Russian oligarch Gavrie Popov's experiments above the Arctic Circle. He hadn't been sure exactly what creatures Popov was breeding in his secret zoo, but if they hadn't been dangerous, the man would have picked a more convenient place to raise them.

And Nick was right about something else. Kai *had* volunteered to go out on this hunt. He had something to prove to himself.

Every other person in the compound had an active role in Popov's experiments, while all Kai did was count things. He was a slight little teetotaler among a robust group of vodka-swilling adventurers. The rest of the group barely acknowledged the guy who inventoried the bottles of drain cleaner.

He needed to prove to them, and himself, that he was more than a bean counter. Besides, how could he return to Japan next year with experiences that were the same as he'd had in every other job? Adventure was way outside his comfort zone, but the time had come to make a little side trip to that destination.

Out in front of them, a seven-meter by seven-meter steel-barred cage sat in the center of the clearing. The gate at one end had been pulled straight up like a guillotine, ready to hurtle down and trap the catch in the cage. A cluster of bananas hung at the end furthest from the open gate.

"The mother has been getting complacent," Nick said. "She's letting the little one wander off away from the herd. My mother was the same way. Look what a mess I turned out to be. Mama Jumbo's going to learn a hard lesson."

Branches swayed on the other side of the clearing. A low, almost sub-sonic rumble filled the air.

"Quiet!" Nick whispered to the men around him.

A tiny mammoth trunk stuck out through the branches. It raised up into an S shape and sniffed the air in several directions. It zeroed in on the bananas hanging in the cage.

A baby woolly mammoth emerged from the leaves. It stood less than two meters tall, which seemed big to Kai, but this youngster would be dwarfed by its massive adult relatives. Shaggy hair covered its body and its ears looked endearingly oversized, as its round head hadn't yet grown the cranial hump the adults displayed. Its big, brown eyes looked at the bananas with longing.

"That's it, little one," whispered Nick. "Go get yourself a snack from the steel-barred pantry."

The mammoth plodded over to the cage opening. It stopped short of the gate and explored the metal bars with its trunk. Then it stretched its trunk through the opening and reached for the bananas. The grasping little tip came up short.

"No cheating," Nick said. "Go in and get it."

The mammoth stepped into the cage. Its hairy tail cleared the gate. It wrapped its trunk around the bundle of yellow prizes.

"Now!" Nick shouted.

One of the men released the rope holding up the cage door. It hurtled down and slammed shut with a clang that echoed through the forest. The startled mammoth hopped up an amazing half-meter and landed on the bottom of the cage with a thud. It raised its trunk to the sky and let loose a panicked trumpeting.

From off in the forest, the mother responded with an ear-splitting sound that bordered on a screech.

Nick jumped to his feet and ran to the cage gate. He threw a locking latch shut.

"Go! Go!" he cried out.

An old Russian Army truck roared to life from a dirt road at the other end of the clearing. The truck's winch screamed to life and a thick, rusty cable snapped tight from out of the obscuring ground litter. The cable pulled. The cage rose and moved forward, riding on a trailer that had been hidden below ground.

The mother mammoth trumpeted again, closer this time. The baby answered with a whimpering cry and tossed itself against the cage bars.

As soon as the trailer was on level ground, the truck came barreling back at it in reverse with one man sitting in the open rear cargo area. The truck jerked to a stop at the trailer. The man jumped out and hooked the trailer to a hitch on the truck. He barked a command and the vehicle sent up four rooster-tails of dirt as the driver floored it in forward gear. The tires bit in and the truck launched down the trail with the trailer in tow.

A tree crashed down into the clearing. From behind it, the mother mammoth charged into the open. Kai had mentally prepared himself to see an elephant. He hadn't prepared himself to see this creature.

The beast was twice as tall as an African elephant and far more muscular, with huge forelimbs supporting broader shoulders. Long, thick, brown hair covered the body save a few spots on the animal's face. Two humps above the eyes gave the beast's head an elongated look. Twin tusks curled on either side of its trunk, not round like an elephant's, more like extended canine teeth, flattened on the sides into opposing sharpened edges.

The ground shook as the massive beast pounded after the retreating cage. Kai decided he'd maxed out his need for animal adventure. Two men beside him shared his sentiments and the three fled for the trail back to the compound.

Nick still stood in the clearing where the cage had been. The mammoth charged straight for him, glaring eyes filled with fury.

Nick took a plastic box from his pocket. He pressed a button on the box.

Four small charges in the canopy of the trees exploded. A heavy mesh net flew down from the treetops and draped over the mammoth's head and neck. The creature cried out in fury and skidded to a stop.

It wasn't enough net to capture the animal. Hell, Kai didn't think there was enough netting on the whole island to capture an adult mammoth. But it was enough to slow and confuse it so the team could escape.

Nick pumped a fist in victory and sprinted for the pickup truck waiting in the woods outside the clearing. Kai and the other men followed him. Behind them, the mammoth roared and spun around the clearing trying in vain to shake the heavy net from its head.

Kai was the last one to jump into the back of the truck. Just as he cleared the tailgate the driver floored it. Kai's last sight of the mammoth was of it hooking the net on a broken tree branch so it could pull the thing free.

He thought that was pretty smart for an animal resurrected from over ten thousand years ago. But he'd been more impressed by the creature's size, speed, and strength. Mama mammoth wasn't happy with Junior getting kidnapped. If she had any maternal instincts, she wasn't going to just let him go.

Kai began a mental review of the weapons and ammunition inventory he'd done last week for the compound. He had a bad feeling they were going to need every round.

CHAPTER TWO

Two weeks later

Like a rare planetary alignment, in the month of June everything seemed to converge in Professor Grant Coleman's favor.

The college semester ended with Grant getting some grudgingly positive feedback from Dean Malley, the annoying head of his department. One of Grant's graduating paleontology students had landed a nice position at the Smithsonian, in part from Grant's glowing recommendation. That student's wealthy father then donated a tidy sum to the Paleontology department in appreciation for the fine job they did instructing his son. It killed Malley to have to thank Grant, which doubled how great Grant felt about the whole thing.

The second big event was the sale of another book. *The Forest of Fire* was a supposedly fictional account of a professor in China finding dragons. Grant told no one about the hair-raising "research" he'd done putting that story together. It was the fourth book he'd written about a college professor who ends up battling giant monsters. He never subtitled them "Inspired by True Events" but he certainly could have, if he wanted to admit he was the professor and giant monsters were real. He preferred to do neither. His publisher loved *Forest*, and said he hoped Grant never ran out of inspirations for his amazing stories. Grant hoped he did run out before his "inspirations" managed to kill him.

The advance for that book meant that his monthly dues to the Ex-Wife Party Fund were up to date and even two months ahead. That left him with no big bills to pay during summer break when his college paychecks paused.

And to put icing on the Grant Happiness cake, he'd been invited to consult on a paleontological dig in Utah with another university, all expenses paid. That started in July.

Every star in the sky seemed to shine on Grant Coleman right now.

To celebrate, he was treating himself to a two-week trip to Hawaii before the Utah dig started. Not the tourist mecca of Oahu, but the Big Island, where the pace was more relaxed and he could visit Volcanoes National Park and see Kilauea volcano up close and personal. Just not too up close.

Grant was all smiles as he checked in at the airport for the first of several legs that would transport him to paradise. He wore an outrageously bright Hawaiian shirt for the occasion, a size larger than normal so it covered his round belly. (Sadly, luaus would keep him from starting that diet he kept promising to begin.) He sported a pair of tan cargo shorts, and a ridiculous straw Panama hat. He bought a brightly colored band to keep his glasses in place, but he was waiting until he got to the island to put that on. He even paid the extra fee to check his bag, putting his trepidation of the airline losing it behind the feeling of freedom by not dragging it around. Then he breezed through security and found himself with enough time for a coffee and a cinnamon roll before he had to board his flight. The day could not get better.

While he waited for the cinnamon roll shop's employee to call his name to pick up his cup of caffeine and sugar rush, a voice behind him asked, "Aren't you Grant Coleman?"

He turned around to see a college-aged boy in faded jeans and a long-sleeve T-shirt with a cartoon T-rex on the front. The lettering underneath read I'M HAPPY AND I KNOW IT, BUT… The thin kid looked borderline malnourished and had curly brown hair.

"Are you a process server?" Grant said.

"No."

"Then yes, I'm Grant Coleman. Were you in one of my classes?"

"Gosh, no. I've read all your books. I'm your biggest fan."

Every movie Grant had ever seen where a character uttered the phrase "I'm your biggest fan" had ended up being a horror film. The giant monster books he'd written weren't his greatest source of pride, anyway. He'd written the first one because he was broke. He'd just survived an attack by killer bats during an expedition in a cave, and wrote the truth of it as if it were fiction. The royalties had kept a roof over his head.

He'd much rather have been recognized for his paleontological work.

"I'm glad you enjoyed them," Grant said. "Nice to meet you."

"Nice to meet you" was the politest way he knew to walk away from a conversation. Then the shop employee called his name and Grant was thrilled to step away from the kid to pick up his order. He grabbed his coffee and bun from the counter. He turned around and the kid was still right next to him.

"I'm Connor Rigney." He held out his hand to shake Grant's. Grant shrugged with a coffee in one hand and a boxed cinnamon roll in the other.

"Oh, yeah," Connor said. "Full hands."

The kid was going to need a bigger hint that he needed to get lost. Grant made his way to a tiny table for one in the food court. He sat down and arranged his coffee and food container in such a way as they left no extra usable space.

Connor grabbed a chair from the table next to his and pulled it over. He dropped his red backpack on the floor. A collection of patches from a bunch of National Parks were sewn onto the face of the pack. He sat down opposite Grant and slid Grant's coffee to the left so he could rest his forearms on the table. Grant sighed.

"I have so many questions," Connor said. "Starting with the hot ones the social media groups can't answer."

"There are social media groups discussing my books?" It had never occurred to Grant to even look for one.

"Oh, yeah. Big time. Even international ones. The first question is, why doesn't the professor get himself in better shape?" Connor asked just as Grant took a 700 calorie-sized bite out of his cinnamon roll.

That's the first question? he thought. *Nothing about dinosaur physiology or the nature of pterodactyls, or how bats echolocate. He wants to know why I'm fat.*

Grant speed chewed his food and swallowed. "He's a very busy professor with a full schedule. He gets back from an adventure and wants to celebrate survival. After starving in a jungle some place for days, fasting when he gets home isn't a priority."

"Huh. Second thing. In *Curse of the Viper King*, those giant spiders, wouldn't they need like real giant flies to eat?"

Grant stopped mid-bite and put the cinnamon roll down. This kid's questions were going to bring up memories that made eating impossible. Fantastic.

"A large predator like that could eat any large prey. There's science that backs up most of the creatures in the stories." Grant made a big deal about checking his watch. "My flight is getting ready to board. I need to hit the restroom before that. I've got to run."

Connor might have invited himself to Grant's table, but no self-respecting person would invite themselves to Grant's urinal. He hoped.

Grant stood up and gave the half-eaten cinnamon roll a longing look. Leaving unfinished food that tasted that good was a criminal offense in Grant's book. He considered taking it on the plane, but that would mean taking it into the restroom. Having rested the box on a urinal while he peed would make the pastry completely unappetizing. He picked the box up and dropped it in a trash can by the table.

He made a beeline for the restroom. Connor wasn't following him. Praise God.

Now he'd be able to avoid subjecting himself to the confines of an aircraft restroom during his flight. On his way in, he passed one man on his way out. There wasn't anyone else there. He stood at a center urinal and proceeded with business.

Two men in dark suits and sunglasses entered the bathroom. They had the builds of NFL linebackers.

One of them stopped in the doorway and slid a CLOSED FOR CLEANING sign into place. The other headed for Grant.

Whatever was about to go down, Grant wanted nothing to do with it. He closed the show midstream and tried to zip his pants back up. The zipper stuck. He yanked it twice to no avail. Knowing he was running out of time, he turned to leave with his fly open. He practically ran into one of the men.

"Whoa, excuse me." Grant stepped sideways.

The man moved to block him.

"Doctor Coleman," the man said. It sounded more like an accusation.

"Me? No. My name's Jack. Just a random vacationer. My flight's boarding and I really have to—"

The man grabbed Grant by both shoulders. It felt like if he exerted a newton more pressure, Grant's bones would break. He squeezed in and Grant wasn't going anywhere.

The other man left his station at the doorway. He pulled a large syringe from inside his coat and pulled the cap off the needle with his teeth.

"Oh my God," Grant said. "How did you get that past TSA?"

The man stepped beside Grant and aimed the needle at Grant's neck.

"Look, really, whatever this is, it's a mistake," Grant said. "I don't even know—"

The needle plunged into Grant's neck with all the finesse of a prisoner shivving a guard. Before he could react to the pain, his body went limp. Then the lights in the room dimmed, and then went out.

***

Grant woke up on a cold metal floor. The high noise level and the slight jostling told him he was on an airplane. He guessed it wasn't going to Hawaii. He cleaned some dirt from his glasses. There were crates around him. Most of the stencils on the outside were in a foreign language with a number of reversed letters.

He got to his feet and had to hold on to a crate to keep his balance. Whatever that agent-of-evil in the restroom had injected him with hadn't quite worn off.

He staggered to the front of the aircraft. Gray quilted insulation covered the sides but it wasn't doing much to keep heat in or noise out. Three people sat against the bulkhead. None looked happy.

At the far end a college-aged young man with a shaved head snoozed against the bulkhead. The tip of his long, full beard brushed against his chest with each bob of his head. He wore a Led Zeppelin T-shirt from the 1978 World Tour. Grant wondered if even the kid's parents had been born when that happened. Sleeves of tattoos covered both arms. The kid woke up and squinted at Grant.

In the middle sat a man a few years younger than Grant. A weak chin and a receding hairline gave the poor man a kind of mole-like appearance. He stared at his hands with sadness in his eyes as he fumbled with an empty energy bar wrapper. He wore a golf shirt, khakis, and a set of leather loafers, sans socks.

The third person was a woman in her early 30s who wore jeans, a blue golf shirt with a company logo on the chest and heavy-duty work boots. Her short blonde hair was suffering from a severe case of bed head. She looked up at Grant.

"Well, Sleeping Beauty is finally awake."

"Where am I?"

"On a plane flying to the Arctic Circle with the rest of the kidnapped."

"What the hell for?"

"Don't you know? We're on our way to capture woolly mammoths."

"Hell, no," Grant said. "I have tickets to Hawaii."

"That's good news," she said as she looked over his flowery Hawaiian shirt, "because if you always dressed like that, I'd really feel sorry for you."

Grant had managed to cultivate an intense dislike for this woman after just a few minutes, an act that would normally take an hour. He was going to congratulate her on her achievement when the other man extended his hand.

"Hi, I'm Dr. Marcus Wellstone."

Grant shook his hand. "Dr. Grant Coleman. I'm a paleontologist. Are you as well?"

"No, I'm a medical doctor. Anesthesiology."

Normally, medical doctors flaunted their credentials to people with academic doctorates the way a professional sous chef would compare career choices with a fast-food fry cook. But Marcus didn't sound that way at all. At least one of these three wasn't a jerk.

"I'm Ayaan Kaur," the young man in the Zeppelin shirt said. "IT and computers."

That was the exact level of interaction Grant expected from a computer geek. He was going to be a lot of fun.

A hand touched Grant's shoulder. He turned to see Connor.

"Hey, Grant!"

Grant's jaw went slack. "Connor! What the hell are you doing here?"

"Well, I saw two dudes doing the *Weekend at Bernie's* routine with you coming out of the bathroom in the airport. I went over to stop them and they told me in no uncertain terms to mind my own business. Then I told them it was my business because I was your assistant at the dig you were flying to. One of them pulled a gun and told me that if that was true, I needed to come with them."

"Why didn't you tell them it wasn't true then?"

"I thought, what the hell. I'm kind of between jobs, and this sounded like one of the adventure stories you write."

"I thought you were a paleontologist?" the bitchy woman said to Grant.

"He is," Connor said. "But he also writes kaiju adventure books. *Cavern of the Damned, Monsters in the Clouds, Curse of the Viper King*. They are freaking awesome."

"Kaiju?" the woman asked.

"Giant monsters," Connor said.

"Monsters? How high-brow."

"Oh, yeah. Super cool adventures, like old Godzilla movies, but not as cheesy."

"Not *as* cheesy," she observed. "What praise."

"They're written for fun to entertain people," Grant explained.

Actually, they were written to try to exorcise the nightmares from the previous adventures he had been on. But he sure wasn't sharing that tidbit.

"Paleontology is my actual profession," Grant continued. "What's yours that brings you here?"

"I'm Deborah Becker. I run a specialty engineering firm. Bridges, planes, buildings. You name it, we upgrade it to whatever dumb idea the client has come up with."

"What does that have to do with woolly mammoths?"

"Damned if I know."

The door at the front of the cargo area opened, revealing a carpeted luxury compartment with overstuffed reclining seats and a wide screen TV on the front bulkhead. Soccer players in red and white dashed across a bright green field on the TV. The smell of freshly made coffee wafted out into the cargo area.

Then the last person in the world Grant wanted to see stepped into the cabin.

CHAPTER THREE

The man who entered the cabin wore a tan safari-type shirt and jeans. He had about ten years on Grant, but looked like he'd spent those ten years pumping iron in the gym and re-hydrating at juice bars. Though his hair looked naturally dark, a bit of gray speckled his neatly trimmed beard and moustache. Even the scar under one eye made him ruggedly attractive instead of disfigured. All those good looks would have been enough to have Grant despise a stranger on sight. But since this man was Angelo Destro, Grant had many more reasons.

Destro had taken the profession Grant loved and remade it into an evil twin. Destro peddled fossils on the black market to the highest bidder. Whether he acquired the artifact by stealing it from a museum or illegally digging it from the ground made no difference to him. If he sold it to a drug kingpin or a murderous warlord, that made no difference to him, either. All that mattered was the payout.

But as far as Grant was concerned, the worst offense Destro had committed had been taking Grant's college friend Mike Rabon under his wing. Mike had been on his way to becoming a great paleontologist under the right guidance. Instead, he became a black marketeer under Destro, the world's worst role model. Mike had been with Grant on his recent expedition to China in search of dragons. He hadn't made it home.

"Destro, you bastard," Grant said.

"Grant Coleman," Destro said. "Great to see you up and at 'em. Have a nice rest?"

"You know kidnapping is against the law, right?"

"Laws are guidelines for stupid people to follow. The wiser of us are not bound by their strictures."

"People will be looking for me when I go missing."

"I know you," Destro said. "No, they won't."

"Well, maybe not right away," Grant said. "But someone probably will, eventually. And for these people as well."

"Everyone else here volunteered." Destro faced the rest of the group. "Didn't you?"

Grant looked at the other three. Ayaan had a smile on his face. But Marcus and Deborah both gave a glum-faced nod.

"Well, I sure as hell didn't volunteer," Grant said.

"No, Mike Rabon did," Destro said. "And when you didn't bring him back from China with you, that volunteered you to take his place."

"He didn't come back from China because the greed you instilled in him got him killed."

"However it happened, it left you as my second choice. Congratulations."

Grant was the last person to ever instigate a fight, but Destro had it coming. But he also had about twenty pounds of muscle more than Grant. Grant looked around and saw a shovel in a bundle of other tools. He reached for it.

The bulky thug from the airport bathroom stepped up behind Destro. His eyes burned a hole through Grant. Grant put his hand back in his pocket.

"Time for a quick briefing on our little mission," Destro said. "We are on our way to Mammoth Island, or at least that's what the Russians called it. It's in supposedly international waters in the sea between Canada and Russia. I'm sure that you all remember the news stories around finding a complete frozen baby woolly mammoth in Siberia a few years back?"

Grant did. Russians had chopped the thing out of the ice in a block and then flown it out underneath an old Russian military helicopter. Where it went after that had never been very clear.

"Well, Gavrie Popov, a Russian oligarch with whom I've had many profitable business deals, bought that mammoth popsicle and has spent the intervening years bringing a facsimile of that creature back to life. Mammoth Island is home to his lab."

"And you think we're going to help him out?" Grant said.

"Not at all. Despite me getting him a line on that furry carcass, and despite all the great finds I'd funneled his way over the years, my Russian pal refused to cut me in on this deal. So, I'm cutting myself in on it. We are going to bring home a woolly mammoth from his island."

"You know he has one?"

"He has several. The operation is a complete success. That's why now is the time to strike."

"We're going to land and he's going to hand over a mammoth to us?" Deborah said.

"Absolutely not. That's why I had Mr. Williams behind me here parachute in a team of his specialists yesterday to secure the lab and ensure compliance. No one there will put up a fuss as I take what's rightfully mine."

"You had the scientists there murdered?" Grant said. "Even for you that's a new low."

"As long as they complied with orders, they were merely detained. Once we land, all of you will have roles to play. Deborah will make sure that we have a way to safely bring our woolly cargo home. Dr. Marcus will sedate our cargo. Ayaan will copy and then delete all the research records."

"Erasing them out of spite?" Grant said.

"I'll make them available to Gavrie," Destro said, "for a fair price. Unless someone else outbids him."

"You never miss a trick, do you, Destro?"

Destro smiled and addressed the rest of the group. "Dr. Coleman and his assistant, Connor, will be our resident mammoth experts."

Grant started to say that the only things Connor knew about extinct creatures were pseudo-facts he'd read in pulpy giant monster books. The poor kid didn't know what he was getting into, and Grant wanted to get him off the hook. But once Destro considered the kid extra baggage, what would he do with him? He might eject him to lighten the load. Grant opted to keep his mouth shut.

"The two mammoth men will be asking the onsite staff all the right questions," Destro continued, "so I can keep our bundles of joy alive and healthy after we get them out of there."

"Bundles?" Grant said.

"Even Noah knew to take two of everything onto the ark. Now we'll be landing soon, so everyone stay seated."

Destro closed the door and left the five of them in the cabin.

"Is he right that you all volunteered?" Grant said. He turned to Deborah. "You said you were kidnapped."

"Kidnapped. Blackmailed. What's the difference?"

"About ten years in Federal sentencing guidelines. What did he have on you for blackmail?"

"A full tyrannosaurus skull," Deborah said. "I bought it from him for display at my firm. It's a fixture in the lobby. He threatened to expose that all the paperwork was fake. It would ruin my business' reputation."

"And you, doc?"

"Fossilized eggs," Marcus said. "I bought a whole nest."

"So, that's probably not a crime that would send you to jail."

"The money I used to pay for the eggs probably would, though. There may have been some double-billing involved."

"For the love of..." he turned to Ayaan. "And you really did volunteer?"

"I'm an IT mercenary," Ayaan said. "I follow the money to the next employer since job security is like smoke in the wind these days. Destro paid good, half in advance. Plus, he said I'd get to see a real woolly mammoth. Who wouldn't want to do that?"

"People who want to live a long healthy life, that's who."

The plane's engines throttled back and the aircraft made a bank to the left and then leveled out. Hydraulics churned as flaps and landing gear extended for touchdown.

Grant found a crate tied down with two cargo straps. He sat beside it and wrapped his arms through the straps. Connor sat down beside him.

"Thanks for not giving me up back there," Connor said. "I got the vibe that that guy might kill me if he knew my last real job was delivering pizzas."

"I've known Destro a long time. He's an untrustworthy, egotistical, pretentious pile of crap. Keep your head down and don't cross him."

"Will do. And I'll be a help to you, I swear."

"Start with not getting yourself killed."

Grant closed his eyes and wished that he was still lying asleep in his bed and that all of this was a bad dream brought on by poor sleep and too many late night snacks. His alarm would sound and he'd see that all of this had been a nightmare.

But history told him he never got off that easy.

CHAPTER FOUR

With no windows in the cargo area, Grant startled when the aircraft's tires made a screeching, bouncing touchdown on a runway. As the plane taxied to a stop, he came to the awful realization that he was north of the Arctic Circle and dressed for Hawaii.

He stood up and looked around the cabin. Several suitcases were piled in one corner. None of them were his. Having his suitcase here wouldn't have done him much good anyway. It was filled with shorts and T-shirts. He hadn't even packed a jacket. He thought the daily low would be 72 degrees, not 72 degrees below zero.

The door to the forward cabin opened and Williams entered the cargo area carrying an AK-47 assault rifle. He went straight for the rear of the plane. Destro appeared in the doorway with a concerned look on his face and another AK-47 in his hands.

"Guns?" Grant said. "What kind of reception are we getting here at Ice Station Zebra?'

"Shut up, Grant," Destro said. "I don't need your usual smart-ass commentary on this trip."

"Then you should have let me go to Hawaii. Smart-ass is the only commentary I do."

The second thug from Grant's restroom kidnapping stepped out of the cabin. He also had an AK-47.

"Sonoma," Destro said. "Hold up here."

The man nodded.

"You hired mercenaries named Williams and Sonoma?" Grant said.

"I hired mercenaries who used the cover names Williams and Sonoma to maintain anonymity. The way you should have used a pen name to write your stupid giant monster books."

Grant couldn't decide whether to be impressed or humiliated that Destro knew about his books.

Williams hit a big black button on the bulkhead and a set of stairs lowered down from the aircraft's tail. Grant tucked his knees to his chin and braced himself for a blast of cold air and a case of frostbite.

The stairway lowered, and a rush of warm air blew into the cargo area. Daylight lit the interior of the plane. Williams disappeared down the steps. A few minutes later Williams reentered the cargo area.

"No one's here," he said to Destro. "But the lab is safe to enter."

"Dammit. Okay, everyone out. Now."

Williams trotted back down the steps. No one else moved. Grant was in no hurry to go someplace where Destro thought he'd need armed security. Destro looked at the immobile group and his face went red.

"Go! Get off the plane!"

The five stood up. Deborah looked at Grant, waiting for him to take the lead.

"Oh no," Grant said. "Ladies first, I insist. In my experience, in these situations, being at the head of the line never pays off."

"What bravery," she said with a sneer.

She pushed past Grant and descended the steps. Ayaan shouldered a light backpack and followed her with the blasé attitude of a man on the way to a bus stop. Dr. Marcus exhaled a resigned sigh, and followed. Connor stepped up next to Grant with a smile on his face, like a dog waiting for a treat.

Grant shook his head. This hero-worship routine was already feeling pretty old. He descended the steps with the young man in tow. Destro followed them, with Sonoma covering the rear.

Grant stepped out into a surprisingly pleasant environment. The air had a touch of a chill and nearly no humidity, but the temperature was downright pleasant. A thin haze turned the sun into a glowing disc. The lumpy asphalt runway the plane sat on had been paved in the center of an alpine meadow. All around them, the ground rose into hills carpeted with a forest of pines.

"Did we land in the wrong place?" Grant said.

"No," Destro said. "This island is a hot bed of geothermal activity. Enough heat is vented to push back the cold in this valley. The twenty-four-hour summer sun doesn't hurt, either."

"How does someone keep a place like this secret?" Connor said.

"The warm water vapor rising into colder air puts it in perpetual cloud cover to keep it hidden. Plus, it's surrounded by sea ice, so until global warming breaks that up, no one will be sailing by and bumping into it. Popov built a geothermal reactor under the lab, so he has power while being off the rest of the world's grid."

Williams led the group to a low, concrete block building off the side of the runway. It was the size of a suburban strip mall, but had very few windows and only one set of metal double doors that Grant could see.

A simple corrugated metal warehouse stood on the other side of the building. Behind both rose a reinforced, seven-meter-high chain link fence. At the top, an overhang of razor wire pointed away from the building and toward the woods. The support posts were as wide as telephone poles, the chain links in the mesh twice as thick as normal but with much wider openings. The fence stretched out in both directions and seemed to encircle the clearing that hosted the airstrip and building.

"Someone was serious about keeping everyone in this compound from getting out," Marcus said.

"Not the way that razor wire is pointed," Deborah said. "They were serious about keeping something on the outside from getting in."

Williams took them into the building. Sonoma stayed outside at the door. Just like the fencing, Grant wasn't sure if he was keeping them in or keeping someone else out.

The first room was small, not much more than a vestibule or maybe a changing room. They passed through another door and entered a laboratory.

The place had been impressive at one point. Rows of workstations, each with its own set of computers, monitors, and state of the art scientific equipment. Centrifuges, gas chromatographs, test tubes, pipettes. The place had been a researcher's dream.

But now it was a nightmare. Much of the equipment had been smashed. Glass shards littered the floor. Monitors sat cock-eyed on broken stands. Even some of the chairs for the workstations had shattered legs.

The worst part was the dried blood. Splattered on walls. Pooled in corners. Streaked across the floor. A number of people had died horribly in this room.

Destro took in the scene and looked angry. "Son of a bitch. Williams, did Ward's team do this?"

"Those weren't the orders. They were told to preserve all the tech."

"Does this look preserved to you? And where the hell is his team?"

"No clue."

"You and Sonoma need to find them. Now."

Williams left the building and called for Sonoma to follow him.

"Maybe you can give us a few details on what's going on?" Deborah said.

"Ward's advance team parachuted in and was supposed to hold Popov's scientists for us until we got here. Something went wrong because the scientists aren't here and neither is Ward's team."

"Ward's team didn't check in when they arrived?" Grant said.

"Radio silence planned, for obvious reasons."

"They sure got the silence part right. Maybe they just dislike you as much as I do and don't want to chat."

Destro charged Grant and shoved him up against the wall. The look in his eyes said he was out for blood.

"What did I say about being a smart-ass? A reminder here that everyone on this island with a gun works for me, and I have the only means to get home. I recommend you shut up before I decide your assistant probably knows enough to get the job done and your role here isn't that important after all."

Grant realized he'd pushed the overstressed black marketeer a bit too far for the circumstances.

"I get it," he said.

Destro let him go and stepped away. A little of the fury drained from his face. He turned to the rest of the group.

"We'll get this job done anyway," he said. "Deborah, there are transport cages stored in the warehouse behind this building. Figure out how to modify one and get it on the plane with a mammoth inside. Dr. Marcus, medical supplies are kept in the store room at the far end of this building. Make me a cocktail to at least get a mammoth drowsy, preferably asleep. Ayaan, find a working computer and download all the research you can find."

He turned back to Grant. "And you and Connor need to dig through this lab and find out what makes a mammoth tick. If the one we capture doesn't make it back home alive, neither will you."

CHAPTER FIVE

Grant turned to Connor and spoke into his ear in a low voice. "Get busy with a broom and clean us up a place to work. Keep far away from Destro and his men."

"You got it," Connor said.

Grant followed Ayaan to the rear of the lab where a smashed laptop sat hooked up to a cracked monitor.

"You can get the files we need out of this mess?" Grant said.

Ayaan swept a collection of broken lab equipment off a counter and slung his backpack there in its place. He unzipped it and poured out a laptop and a collection of devices and cables Grant had never seen before.

"Dude, nothing's so damaged I can't find something on it. But no point in starting the search here. Always go to the source."

Ayaan took his laptop over to what looked like a big metal wardrobe. The double doors had huge dents in them. He opened them to reveal several rows of computer servers and a snake's den of wires running between them. Two of the servers looked damaged. Ayaan dropped a built-in shelf from one side and set his laptop on it. He sighed.

"Total cluster in here. Nothing's labeled. One of these servers is a certified antique. It's like they had a schizophrenic IT designer."

"Anything with mammoth in the title is what I'll need first," Grant said.

"You know," Ayaan said as his laptop booted up, "Angelo didn't seem like such a jerk before we left."

"I could have told you different."

Ayaan didn't look up from the computer as he worked. "Dude, like I didn't realize that he was going to kidnap you. He said everyone was totally volunteering for this expedition."

"And it turns out only you were. Your lesson here is to never trust Angelo Destro."

"Way ahead of you on that one."

"We'll poke around to see what else is going on," Grant said.

Grant joined Connor as the kid swept the floor around a large lab table. A glass tray with a resealable lid sat in the corner. Inside, something rectangular floated in a murky liquid. Grant checked the hand-written label on the side of the tray.

Sample 3462
Mammuthus homicidus

Connor dropped his red backpack on the floor and leaned in to peer at the container. "What does *Mammuthus homicidus* mean?"

"Latin name for a species. The first is the genus for the entire mammoth family, but the grim-sounding *homicidus* species name is a new one."

He popped open the lid. The stink of preserving alcohol hit him in the face and he blinked and recoiled. The smell dissipated and he turned back to look inside.

A hunk of fat floated inside. It still held the skin on the top side. The skin was covered with long, coarse hair. Grant grabbed a pen from the desk and then moved some of the hair aside. Underneath was a finer coat of shorter hair. An outer covering of long guard hairs and a shorter undercoat was exactly what woolly mammoth specimens had. But this wasn't thawed out ten-thousand-year-old hair. It was new, with a rich brown color and recently active root follicles. And the fat didn't have the desiccation associated with long-term freezing.

"This isn't from a mammoth dug out of the ice," Grant said. "This sample came from a living creature."

He gave the guard hairs a closer look. They were very thick, closer to porcupine quills than mammalian hair.

He re-covered the tray and made his way over to Ayaan, who looked completely engrossed by his computer monitor screen.

"Anything interesting in there?"

"The most interesting thing is that this top-secret operation used no encryption. Not even a password."

Connor stepped up and looked over Ayaan's shoulder.

"I'm guessing they didn't ever have visitors," Connor said, "and hundreds of kilometers of ice was an acceptable firewall."

"And no one was going to hack in," Ayaan said. "This place has no internet connection, isn't even built to have one."

"The ultimate security," Grant said. "What have you found so far?"

"Dude, you have no idea. I'm digging into the files with Mammuthus in the titles. They've been working on this for years. They have records of generations of clones and clone descendants. This is going to totally blow-up science."

"There's a fresh specimen on the table over there. You said there are generations?"

"Definitely."

"Now the fence makes more sense," Grant said. "They let the mammoths run free on the outside while they stayed safe on the inside."

"I sorted the files by date and copied some of the earliest ones."

Ayaan pulled a thumb drive from his laptop and plugged it into a tablet. He tapped the tablet screen and it came to life, populated with a dozen or so file folders. He handed it to Grant.

"Apparently not everyone here spoke Russian," Ayaan said. "I copied you the English versions. Enjoy yourself."

"Connor," Grant said, "explore the rest of the lab. Touch as little as possible and let me know what you find."

"You bet!"

The poor kid was clearly dying for something to do. Grant took a seat at a lab bench and began to read through some files. Twenty minutes later, he could not believe what he'd been reading.

"What have you found?" Destro said as he walked up behind Grant.

"Wonderful news if you have a death wish," Grant said. "The accepted extinction date for mammoths is about 10,000 years ago. An isolated species on Wrangel Island could have survived until about 4,000 years ago. Your pal Popov was working with a frozen carcass from the Siberian tundra that was less than 3,000 years old."

"Three thousand years? That means that while Egyptian pharaohs were building pyramids, woolly mammoths were still walking through Asia. That's a hell of an overlap."

"The accepted theory is that hunting pressure from Neanderthals and early man was a contributing factor to the specie's extinction."

"There's no way mammoths could have survived against Bronze Age hunters," Destro said.

Connor returned and listened in on the conversation.

"*Mammuthus primigenius*, your basic woolly mammoth, did not," Grant said. "What Popov's people were resurrecting was a new species they called *Mammuthus homicidus*. It had specific adaptations to deal with the increasing threat of predators. Human predators."

"Such as?"

"It was bigger, by about 50 percent. About six meters tall, maybe nine metric tons. Reinforced skull. Tusks look absolutely lethal. No longer rounded, they are more like extended canines, narrow, with sharp edges on both sides, like a sword."

"That's like something straight out of one of your books," Connor said.

"Darwin would have been proud of their evolution," Grant said. "This mammoth would have been a formidable beast to try to take down with spears and bronze axes. These idiots didn't resurrect a docile woolly mammoth. They picked the one version that comes upgraded for combat with tusks like scimitars. I'll bet it was more dangerous than Popov bargained for."

"You're sure about all this?" Destro said.

"The data is all here. This is a new species."

"Fantastic! That just doubled my price. I can see a real bidding war heating up for a new species."

"Did you hear what I said?" Grant asked. "This thing would not only stomp us to death, it could cut us up into little shreds."

"I have a team here on the island to take care of capturing it. You just need to keep it alive after that. Why don't you find out what to feed it and let me worry about the rest?"

Destro walked away.

Connor looked up at Grant. "If it was me, I wouldn't mess with one of those mammoths."

"Neither would I."

CHAPTER SIX

Williams led a man in black fatigues into the lab. The man was of average height, but his oversized chest told of hours of steroid-enhanced gym workouts. He had an AK-47 slung from one shoulder and a belt full of ammunition magazines around his waist. Dirt and sweat caked his face. He looked relieved to see Destro.

"A new player has entered the game," Grant said.

Williams and the man met Destro in the middle of the lab. Grant stepped over to hear their conversation.

"Get prepared for bad news," Williams said.

"Ward!" Destro said to the man beside Williams. "Where the hell is the rest of the team?"

"The ones who are left are watching the perimeter of the airstrip."

"The ones who are left? Where are Popov's scientists?"

"This place was deserted when we got here, everything torn to hell like this. Sears and Penny are walking the perimeter fence. I sent the rest of the team out to search the area for Popov's people. They haven't come back yet."

"Radio them and see where they are."

"No answer from the few radios we brought. We weren't supposed to need radios. The plan was that we parachute in and secure the lab. You arrive the next day and we all fly home. We weren't supposed to be scouring the woods for anyone."

"Fair enough. Let's go to the roof and keep a watch out for that patrol while the rest of these people get a handle on Popov's operation in here."

"Roger that."

Williams and Ward left the lab. Destro noticed that Grant was watching him.

"What are you looking at?" Destro said.

"If I said absolutely nothing," Grant replied, "would you be offended?"

"The clock's ticking, Coleman. You'd better be ready to nursemaid some mammoths soon." Destro headed out the door.

Connor joined Grant as soon as Destro left. "There's something over here you need to see. I thought you'd want to check it out before Destro did."

Connor walked Grant over to the far end of the lab and a big silver door to what looked like a walk-in freezer. The temperature gauge beside the door was cracked and the needle was missing. Connor pulled open the door. Cold air blew out and hit him in the face.

"I'm spitting distance from the North Pole," he said, "and there's a generator nearby making power to run a freezer. Totally bizarre."

Racks of frost-encrusted plastic boxes filled the freezer. He brushed clean a label to reveal that they were categorized as mammoth samples.

"More mammoth samples," Grant said. "Some are pretty old."

"There's more in here than just mammoth," Connor said as he pointed to the far end of the freezer.

The frozen corpse of a small man sat in the corner. He was curled up in a ball, as if trying to ward off the cold. A layer of frost dusted his body and a tiny icicle hung from the tip of his nose.

Grant stepped closer. Checking for a pulse obviously wasn't necessary. The man wore a lab coat over jeans. He looked about fifty with close cropped hair. Grant guessed he had been one of the scientists working here. He gave the body a nudge with the toe of his shoe. It was frozen solid.

"That kind of a solid freeze would take a long time for such a dense mass starting out at 98 degrees," Grant said.

"Why would he let himself freeze to death in here?"

"Because that must have been a better fate than what happened to the rest of Popov's people who stayed out there."

Grant's teeth chattered. Either the cold was starting to chill him to the bone in his tropical outfit, or being next to a frozen corpse was giving him the creeps. He'd accept either reason.

"Let's get out of here," Grant said.

Connor stepped back into the lab. Grant backed out of the freezer and slammed the door behind him. His glasses immediately fogged over. He took them off and cleaned them with his shirt.

An indistinct shape approached him. He put his glasses back on and Marcus came into focus.

"You look frosty," Marcus said.

"One of the scientists from this lab is in that freezer. It looks like he was hiding and froze to death."

"Damn. That team Destro sent in must have terrified him."

"It takes a long miserable time to freeze to death. He was hiding from something else, the same something that went through this lab like a tornado. Did you find anything to keep us from resorting to freeze-drying as a defense?"

"Well, seems they have everything I'd need to tranquilize a large animal," Marcus said. "Depending on how big it is."

"What's the biggest thing you ever put to sleep?"

"A three-hundred-pound woman."

"Bump that dosage up by a factor of sixty."

Marcus' jaw dropped. "That would make a mammoth…"

"Freaking huge."

Deborah re-entered the lab and stepped over to Grant and Marcus. "You two need to come see what I found outside."

She led them out to the rear of the lab. A row of a dozen large cages with thick iron bars and concrete floors paralleled the back of the building. All were empty.

"Looks like someone closed the zoo already," Grant said.

"Or maybe the cages were always empty," Marcus said, "and the scientists never made a mammoth, and we can go home."

"No, there are tissue samples in the lab from woolly mammoths. But these cages, big as they are, could not have held an adult mammoth."

"They couldn't even hold what they were supposed to," Deborah said.

She led them down to the end cage. The door had been ripped from the hinges and lay on the grass several meters from the cage.

"Looks like the prisoner broke out," Grant said.

"Not quite," Deborah said. She stepped over and pointed to the deformed bars in the center of the door. "This wasn't pushed out. It was pulled off. Whatever was in here was liberated."

"Like someone wrapped a chain around the bars and pulled," Marcus said.

"Except there isn't a scratch on the paint," Deborah said.

The grass around the door was trampled flat. Grant walked past the door to the fence. He looked down the fence to the west. Halfway to the end, a section had collapsed inward.

"So," Grant said, "let's say you're a mother woolly mammoth, and someone stole Junior and put him in a cage. What would your response be?"

"I'd say something like this," Marcus said.

"Momma crushed the fence and then pulled off a jailbreak," Grant said.

Deborah thumped the side of one of the fence support poles. "Do you know how powerful a mammoth would need to be to get through this fence?"

"Elephants in the wild push over enormous trees to get to the leaves at the top. This mammoth would have a much stronger motivation and much more muscle mass."

A burst of gunshots sounded from the forest. A man in black fatigues like Ward's jumped over the collapsed fence and into the compound. He came running in the group's direction, frantically waving his AK-47.

"Run!" he shouted. "Run!"

Experience had taught Grant that when someone yelled run, it was best to just assume they had a good reason, and then sprint in the opposite direction.

But before he could turn and bolt, one of the trees behind the fleeing mercenary crashed down over the flattened fence. It sent up a cloud of pine needles and dirt. A trumpeting roar filled the air.

Then a woolly mammoth stepped into the compound.

CHAPTER SEVEN

The creature was just as large as Grant had feared it would be. The mammoth towered more than twice as tall as an African elephant and was much more massive, with a swollen and elongated skull and huge forelimbs. Except for a few spots near the eyes and mouth, long, thick, brown hair covered the body.

The mammoth raised its trunk to the sky and trumpeted. The noise resembled an elephant call, but with an added shriek that made Grant's blood run cold. And raising its head was the perfect way to show off the great curling tusks on either side of its trunk. They were as the records described: flattened like a sword with twin sharpened edges.

The mercenary half-turned without stopping. He aimed from the hip and sent a hail of bullets back at the mammoth. With its huge size and close proximity, the mercenary could hardly miss. The bullets struck the beast all along its body. Except for a small flash on impact, the rounds had no effect on the creature at all. It spied the fleeing mercenary and charged in pursuit.

Grant had never seen such a large creature move so quickly. All the grace associated with an elephant was replaced with the power of a charging rhino. The mercenary wasn't going to outrun it.

The others ran back into the lab building. Grant was the last one at the door. He looked back in the vain hope that the man in black might make it as well.

The mercenary was still fifty meters away. The galloping mammoth closed on the man. When it was close enough that the man fell into its shadow, it reared its head sideways, and then swung it in a sweeping forward arc. The tusks went through the mercenary like a fork through Jell-O. He exploded in sprays of bright red blood and the two halves of him dropped to the ground.

The mammoth did not pause to savor the victory. Its eyes locked on Grant, and it kept charging past the row of cages.

Grant ducked into the lab and slammed the door behind him. He pressed the tiny button in the middle of the knob to lock the door and immediately felt like an idiot.

Destro ran up to his side.

"What the hell is going on?"

"Good news. We found your mammoth. Why don't you grab a bag of peanuts and go coax it into a cage?"

The ground vibrated as the mammoth ran up along the side of the building. Then there was an enormous crash as something struck the lab. Pictures flew off the wall and glassware slid off tables to shatter on the floor. The mammoth trumpeted in fury.

From the direction of the runway outside of the lab came the whine of starting aircraft engines.

"Oh, hell no," Destro said.

The group crossed the lab and crowded around one of the windows. Outside, the cargo plane had retracted the stairway and the propellers were spinning up to speed.

Destro pulled a handheld radio from the pocket of his cargo pants. He squeezed the thing so hard that the plastic case squeaked.

"Drew, where do you think you're going?"

A voice cracked from the radio speaker. "Someplace safe. There's a giant elephant trying to stomp your building."

"No kidding. That's what we're here to capture."

"After you box it up to take it home, I'll come get it. I'm not going to sit around and become a chew toy for that thing. I just saw it cut a man in half."

The plane made a half-turn and began to taxi down the runway.

"You shut down that goddamn plane right now," Destro said.

"I'm heading back to Yellowknife. I'll give you two days to catch that thing and crate it. I'm not sticking around while you do it, though."

The plane's engines ramped up to full speed and the aircraft accelerated down the runway. Grant prayed the pilot would have a last-second change of heart. But instead, the plane's wheels left the ground and the landing gear retracted.

"Son of a bitch!" Destro shoved the radio back in his pocket. In seconds, the plane disappeared into the clouds.

"Now we're trapped here," Deborah said.

"The good news is all your luggage is still on the plane," Grant said. "So at least that's safe."

The building shook as the mammoth gave it another pounding. Mortar dust drifted down from the wall and the overhead lights blinked on and off. Grant squeezed himself under a desk for protection. Connor crawled under a desk opposite him.

"Can that thing get through the wall?" Connor said

"Imagine a nine-ton wrecking ball covered in fur," Grant said. "Then imagine it's pissed off."

CHAPTER EIGHT

Gunfire sounded from the roof above them.

"Okay!" Destro said. "Looks like Ward's getting in on the fight."

The mammoth roared, but based on how ineffective the other mercenary's bullets had been against the mammoth's defensive fur, Grant thought that the beast sounded more irritated than wounded. The pounding on the building stopped.

More gunfire rained down from the roof. The elephant trumpeted and its footsteps pounded the ground from the area by the cages. Another burst of gunshots. Then something heavy crashed onto the roof and Ward screamed.

Everything went quiet.

Then the wall shook as the mammoth took another shot at knocking it down. This time concrete blocks cracked.

The mammoth trumpeted again. The pounding stopped. A huff sounded outside the building followed by the thud of heavy, retreating footsteps.

Deborah sighed with relief from under the table where she'd taken shelter. She crawled out and stood up. Marcus stood nearby, dusting concrete chips and sand off his shirt.

"Are you okay?" Marcus said.

"No physical damage. Psychologically scarred for life, but no physical damage."

"I hear you on that one," Connor said. "Now I know how one of Dr. Coleman's characters in *Curse of the Viper King* felt trapped by a giant snake in a stone pyramid."

Grant wished this kid had never read any of his books.

"Why do you think it quit?" Marcus said.

"Maybe it decided it couldn't crack this nut," Grant said. "Or maybe it gave itself a headache."

The lights blinked again.

"Destro," Deborah said. "Since we're stuck here for a while, I'm going to find out where our power is coming from. The team here abandoned ship, and it would be nice to make sure the juice keeps flowing without them."

"Good idea. This is the only building and the source is geothermal, so I'd start by heading down." He pointed his rifle at Grant. "You and I are going to the roof to see what happened."

Grant went to the stairwell to the roof and Destro followed him up.

The scene on the roof was grim. Spent brass shell casings littered the black asphalt roofing. The cage door that had been torn from its hinges sat on the roof. Beneath it lay Ward in a wide pool of blood. The only way the cage door could have gotten on the roof was if the mammoth had hurled it.

The idea sent a chill down Grant's spine. Killer mammoths were bad enough. Killer mammoths smart enough to use things as weapons was a new level of nightmare.

#

Deborah saw a metal door to a stairwell in the corner of the lab opposite the one Grant and Destro had taken. Painted on it was a single word in Russian she did not understand over a downward pointing arrow. She headed for that.

She pushed the door open. The warmer air inside the stairwell carried the scent of minerals with a hint of sulfur.

"Nothing says geothermal like a smell reminiscent of Hell," she said to herself.

Deborah let the door close behind her and peered over the edge of the landing. The stairs went down several stories. She began her descent.

Deborah vowed that when she got home, she was going to murder her husband, Tyrone.

He was the impetus behind their dealings with Destro. She'd never cared about fossils. In fact, she'd grown to dread seeing one, especially at work. Finding one onsite generally resulted in delays as paleontologist eggheads got notified and they filed injunctions to have the government declare the excavation their own personal dig.

But Tyrone had never outgrown his childhood dinosaur fascination. He'd gotten both of them in touch with Destro to "get an interesting fossil for the living room" as Tyrone said. That morphed into him buying more behind her back, culminating with him committing to buy the T-Rex skull. It would have blown their personal budget if she hadn't switched the purchase over to her firm and made it the lobby centerpiece. But that big sale had been the leverage Destro needed to get her on this screwed up expedition. And her husband was going to pay for it forever once she got home.

She leaned on the banister as she descended the steps. It rocked in its mounts and she stepped back from it fast. She'd always found that one of the enduring byproducts of the Soviet era was a Russian penchant for slipshod construction. So far, this place was chockful of prime examples: a stairwell that couldn't pass a code inspection in Yemen, the improperly mixed mortar between the blocks that had turned to dust under the mammoth attack, the lumpy runway that had been laid on insufficiently prepped earth. She wondered if a lifetime of enduring poor construction meant that no Russian now knew what good construction was.

The last set of steps ended in a basement larger than the building above it. The stale, hot air threatened to bake her from the inside out. A turbine spun in the center of the room. The old girl would not have looked out of place in a photo of the opening of the Hoover Dam. Pipes of hot air tapped from somewhere below the room fed into the turbine to make it spin and generate electricity. Exhaust pipes exited on the other side and back underground. Rust caked every component, including the pressure relief valves. Empty holes tattled on the pipe fittings' missing bolts. The whole thing looked like a bad high school shop project circa 1960.

She made her way to what looked like an operator work station. The labels were in Russian but the symbols were universal and she could get a good sense of the system. To the left, a stylus recorded the turbine's output on a slow-spinning paper wheel. It had been stable for several days.

She made the long trek back up the stairs as she cursed Popov for not installing an elevator. By the time she got back to ground level, her calves were killing her.

Marcus stood outside the stairway door. Deborah had been the first "volunteer" Destro had collected, and Marcus had been the second. They'd talked a lot while the other team members were "recruited" for the expedition. His eyes darted back and forth and sweat beaded across his extended forehead.

"What did you find?" he said.

"The source of our electricity such as it is. You said you found tranquilizers. You sure you can bring one of these mammoths down before it kills us?"

"Between us? I don't know. I work with humans, not animals. I use a hypodermic, not a giant dart gun. There will be no way to monitor the animal for how it's working." Marcus became more agitated as he continued to speak. "If I overdo it, I'll kill the animal and then one of Destro's men will kill me. If I underestimate the dose, the thing will wake up and kill us all."

"Marcus, relax. All of us are here doing things we'd rather not, and all of us are working outside our comfort zones. But we aren't far outside our areas of expertise. I've never built a giant cage inside an airplane, but I'll figure it out. You've never doped up a mammoth, and you'll figure it out."

Marcus took a deep breath and exhaled hard. "Okay. All I can do is the best I can, right? Worst that can happen is they shoot me."

"Don't worry. Destro will shoot that smart-ass professor long before you."

"Say, why do you have it out for him?"

"I worked my way through college. Days working construction around men who said I didn't belong on the job, then nights under professors who said I wasn't smart enough to belong in college. Once Destro said a college professor was our last pickup, I knew just what we'd get. A know-it-all snob, clueless about the real world and with little useful to offer."

She didn't want to add that Grant being a few pounds shy of morbidly obese didn't win him any points with her either. She took physical fitness as a personal responsibility people shouldn't shun.

"I don't know," Marcus said. "He seems okay. Sure is willing to give Destro a harder time than I'd dare to."

"And if Grant was alone in the cage poking that bear, I'd tell him go have fun. But we're all in the cage and I don't want the bear taking it out on the rest of us. You'll see. When everything goes to hell, he'll be spouting some animal behavior theory while we all get slashed to bits."

She and Marcus went over to Destro and Grant.

"There's a geothermal generator in the basement," she said. "The only reason it's still making power is that luck favors the foolish. Mechanically, I'm amazed it runs, period. Geothermal output has been steady, so it's functioning in some automatic mode without an operator. But if that controller goes off the rails, the system will scram, and we'll be in the dark. Or worse."

"Do I want to know what's worse?" Grant said.

"What's worse is one of the dozen duct-taped safeties or chronically rusted valves fail or the turbine floods. And then *kapow*."

"No building?" Grant said.

"Maybe no valley," Deborah said.

"Then we'd best capture my mammoths pretty damn fast," Destro said.

CHAPTER NINE

Destro ordered everyone to gather around him for updates. Ayaan and Connor joined Grant, Marcus and Deborah. Just then, Williams and Sonoma returned to the lab and made a beeline for Destro.

"The mammoth has retreated out of the compound," Williams said. "We were on the other side of the warehouse when it attacked. It cut down Sears before it started battering the building."

"Find anyone else?" Destro said.

"Penny is in position at the warehouse. That's it. Ward was firing from the roof. Then I watched the mammoth grab the door from a steel cage with its trunk and hurl it at him like a discus thrower. Did he make it?"

"No."

"Tough break. He went down swinging, though."

"Your compassion for your brother-in-arms is so moving," Grant said.

"Shut up, Ivory Tower. We agree to take risks, we know the price might be high. We wait and mourn after we call mission complete."

"That attack only leaves us three men," Destro said.

"Looks like no one counts you as a man," Deborah said to Grant. "I can understand that."

"We'll need a smaller plan," Destro said. "One mammoth plus the research and the location of more creatures will still be worth a fortune."

"In comparison, I consider my life priceless," Grant said.

"I don't," Destro said. He turned to Marcus. "Hey, Dr. Sleepy, did you find a way to knock one of these things out?"

"There are plenty of sedatives back there," Marcus said, "and some tranquilizer guns locked in a rack."

Williams gave his rifle a little wave. "I brought my lock picker."

"There are also sleeping quarters near the storage room," Marcus said. "It doesn't look like the people who were here packed anything before they left."

"From the blood around the lab," Williams said, "it looks more like they were dragged out."

"A mammoth didn't do that," Connor said. "It couldn't fit in the room."

"Hallelujah," Grant said. "More than one kind of island monster. I was going to leave a bad review about this vacation spot, but not now."

"There were a ton of extra files on that server," Ayaan said. "I'll dig into them."

Ayaan went back to his laptop and began tapping away at a keyboard.

"You did see how big that mammoth was?" Grant said. "No way it could fit in the plane."

"At some point," Destro said, "the things are small enough to fit in one of the cages out back. We'll capture one of the smaller ones."

"In case you haven't been watching any National Geographic programs lately," Grant said, "let me remind you that elephants live in a big family group with a protective matriarch. She's always on the verge of being furious, even on her best days. They defend their young as a group and stomp people to death without a second thought. And the mammoth that cut that mercenary in half? Looks like it's way stronger than any elephant on Earth."

"That just means you'll need to work up a pretty good plan to get one," Destro said. "This expedition is my cash out. Everything I've banked over the years got invested in this. No way in hell I'm not seeing this through."

Grant turned to Williams, hoping the mercenary might still be capable of rational thought. "You have a fraction of the men you planned on having here. You can't want to go through with this."

"Sure do," Williams said. "And so do my men. We all got paid a quarter up front and get the rest when we bring a live mammoth home. We are highly trained and ready."

"You mean the ones who are still alive are trained and ready," Grant said.

"Next of kin gets the deceased's cut. We don't deliver, the widows get nothing. All the more reason that we're all in."

He tapped Grant on the chest with the barrel of his rifle.

"And that means so are you," he added.

Grant stepped away from the gun barrel. "Let me say now how happy I am to risk my life for your collective greed."

"That's the spirit," Destro said.

From overhead came the rocketing roar of an aircraft jet engine.

"What the hell?" Destro said.

The group stepped outside the building. A sweptwing Russian fighter plane had just overflown the runway. A second plane screamed by in its wake.

"Son of a bitch," Williams said.

To the south, two lumbering transport planes broke out of the cloud cover. The quad-engine planes were the largest aircraft Grant had ever seen. Big red stars shined from the fuselages.

"Ilyushin IL-76s," Williams said. "Whoever is coming is serious. There could be hundreds of soldiers on those planes."

"No problem for you," Grant said. "With your men being so highly trained and all."

"Popov is very connected," Destro said. "If he lost contact with his people here, he could easily get the military to respond. We need to disappear before they know we're here."

"And go where?" Grant said. "Up into the forest with the mammoths?"

"Stay here and chat it up with Popov and the Russians," Destro said. "They'll shoot you before you can raise your hands to surrender."

Given the options of Russian bullets or woolly mammoth tusks, there was no good choice. Grant figured that the mammoths were likely more open to reason.

"I know where there's a hole in the fence," he said.

CHAPTER TEN

Williams headed for the door with Sonoma by his side. Grant looked around the lab.

"What are you looking for?" Connor said.

"Something to defend myself with. I see nothing. There's no weapons, especially nothing that could take on a nine-ton semi-armored mammoth."

"Destro and his men have guns."

"Now I feel safe," Grant said. "I could also go for a decent meal, or any meal at this point. The last time I ate was a day ago in a place on the other side of the globe."

"I didn't see any food in here."

"I have to say, this resort meets none of my needs."

The two joined the rest of the group and followed the mercenaries out the door.

Williams led them in a spirited jog toward the collapsed fence. He covered the ground with ease. Grant was huffing and puffing after only a few yards. After his last adventure in China, he'd sworn he was going to get in better shape. He wished he'd followed through on that.

The group passed through a patch of grass splashed with drying blood. The two halves of the slaughtered mercenary, Sears, lay in the grass, one to either side. Grant's stomach rebelled at the sight and threatened to send its contents up for a visit. The fact that it was empty wasn't going to stop it. Grant focused on the back of the head of the person in front of him and kept moving.

Penny sprinted in from the warehouse. Williams gave him a three-second, on the run mission briefing. Penny unclipped a machete from his belt and passed it to Williams. Then he took up a position at the end of the group.

At the fallen fence, the group turned right and crossed into the forest. The towering pines were of a variety Grant had never seen, like balsam fir without lower branches and sporting an archaic needle structure. Smaller, scrubby bushes grew in the space between the trees. He wondered if this valley was a time capsule for plants long extinct elsewhere.

Trampled plants and broken branches marked the path the mammoth had used in and out of the compound. Big, round footprints made divots in the ground. Williams led the group up that route.

"Wait," Grant wheezed. "Isn't there a mammoth at the end of this trail?"

"This trail is open," Williams said. "We need to put the most distance between us and the Russians as fast as we can."

As if to reinforce Williams' point, on the runway behind them, tires screeched. Engines roared against thrust reversers as the first of the Russian cargo planes touched down on the asphalt.

Williams sprinted up the mammoth's trail. The group accelerated behind him like a stretching Slinky. Grant moaned and tried to keep up.

Soon the mammoth's path crossed a crystal-clear creek that ran from the top of the valley down to just short of the runway, where it curved and drained at the valley's far end. The wide, rocky banks on either side told of a time when the stream ran much deeper and faster.

Williams led the group upstream. Grant was relieved they'd stopped following the mammoth's trail before they caught up with it. He was less enthusiastic about the increased uphill slope. His calves started to burn and the irregular stones of the creek bed sent his ankles in directions they'd never tried before. He slipped and one foot splashed into the icy water. His cheap beach sneakers were water-tight as a sieve and his toes went numb. He would have cursed Destro to high heaven, but he didn't have the breath to spare.

Williams climbed out of the stream bed and onto what looked like a game trail. He drew his machete. As he moved forward, he chopped away the few stray branches that crowded the trail. The upslope angle increased until Grant was sure he couldn't pull his pear-shaped body another yard. Then Williams delivered them to an outcrop that overlooked the compound. When the last of the group cleared the forest,

Williams stopped and took a knee. The group bunched up behind him.

"Get down!" Penny ordered from the rear of the group.

They all took a knee. Grant collapsed on his butt, chest heaving, heart pounding like a steam boiler about to blow up. He leaned back against a tree as sweat ran down his flushed face. Deborah looked over at him. She looked infuriatingly fresh, despite all the exertion.

"You going to make it?" she said.

"If this is the other option," Grant said, "I'm starting to think being stomped by a mammoth wouldn't be that bad after all. Aren't you tired?"

"I run marathons."

"Of course you would. I keep meaning to sign up for one, but I'd hate to embarrass all the younger runners I'd beat."

"Sure. Those toddlers would be scarred for life." She looked at him with disgust. "At least we spared Hawaiian vacationers from looking at you on a beach."

"You are the queen of the silver linings."

The view of the compound was quite good. The second plane landed and taxied up behind the first. The rear cargo ramp on the first plane lowered. A squad of soldiers jogged down the ramp and formed a defensive ring around the planes.

Then a tall, trim Russian officer walked down the ramp. While the soldiers wore battle fatigues and combat gear, the general wore a formal uniform, complete with a collection of ribbons over his jacket's breast pocket. The mass of medals was so large that it was visible even at this distance.

A portly, shorter man with just a fringe of hair on his round head followed a few steps behind. He wore a suit, but the tie hung loose and his shirt collar was open.

Williams pulled a small set of binoculars from a pocket and raised them to his eyes. He trained them on the plane.

"That's a Russian Air Force general down there," he said. "Do you know who he's with?"

He handed the glasses to Destro. Destro sighted in on the plane.

"That's Popov with him. And he looks like a beaten dog."

"Then maybe he didn't call in the Russian military," Williams said. "They invited themselves and brought him along."

A voice piped up from behind the group. "I'll bet it was more like they dragged him along."

Grant turned to see a Japanese man in tattered clothes standing just uphill of them. Williams and Sonoma both aimed weapons at the small man. He raised his hands.

"Don't waste bullets on me," he said. "You're going to need them."

CHAPTER ELEVEN

"Who are you?" Destro said.

"Kai Nishikawa," he said. "I work here. Who the hell are *you*? You don't belong here."

"We're on an island above the Arctic Circle," Grant said. "Technically, none of us belong here."

"I'm Angelo Destro, one of the American investors," Destro said. "Gavrie Popov invited me down to see the project's progress."

"Invited guests don't bring private soldiers," Kai said as he pointed at Williams and Sonoma.

"The invitation was implied," Destro said.

"You're part of the team that resurrected these mammoths?" Grant said.

"Animals aren't my thing," Kai said. "I don't even have a pet. I'm logistics and bookkeeping."

"What happened down at the lab?" Destro said.

"A total nightmare. I'm in the storage building, checking inventory. I hear mammoths trumpeting, people screaming. I step outside and into chaos. People running everywhere. Charging woolly mammoths running them down. So, I duck right back into the building and bolt the door."

"You didn't let anyone else in?" Connor said.

"Dude, have you seen the distance between the storehouse and the lab? No one made it to my door. A while later, all the noise winds down. I wait a bit and then look outside. I don't see anyone. I don't even see bodies. There's one mammoth lumbering away down the runway, swinging its head back and forth like it's hunting for survivors.

"Well, like no way I want to have that kind of close encounter. I can see where the mammoths breached the fence, and figure I can hide in the forest better than somewhere in these two buildings. So, I stuff a backpack full of protein bars, and then I make a run for it."

The thought of a backpack full of protein bars got Grant's mouth watering. A cheeseburger would be the ultimate right now, but at this point raw kale would be a gift from the gods.

"I saw your plane land earlier," Kai said, "and then take back off. Those aren't your planes returning to the airstrip now?"

"Russian military," Destro said.

"Another group with an implied invitation," Grant said.

"Oh no, they've probably been invited," Kai said. "Popov has brought a Russian air force general named Vatutin here a few times. Called him a silent partner."

"This time General Vatutin brought Popov," Williams said, still looking through his binoculars. "And a platoon of soldiers."

"That's different. There have never been any soldiers here before."

"Well, there are now," Williams said. "Maybe the silent partner is speaking up."

"Before all this went to hell," Kai said, "I was in a meeting discussing whether the mammoths were ready to be taken out of the valley. The scientists here said no."

"And it looks like the general didn't want to take no for an answer," Destro said.

"All the cages and gear to move mammoths are stored in the warehouse," Kai said. "And those planes look big enough to hold one."

"No way that will be easy," Deborah said.

"A mammoth isn't going to walk into the rear of one of those planes," Destro said. "Vatutin didn't bring all those soldiers with him to play a game of soccer. He's going to be sending teams up here to capture one."

"Follow me," Kai said. "I've got a safe place."

The three mercenaries looked to Destro for confirmation.

Destro nodded. "Follow him."

Kai led them up the hillside along a trail far too narrow for the mammoths to have made. After a half hour, the trail dead ended at a granite cliff.

"How is this a safer place?" Grant said.

"It isn't." Kai pointed up. "Up there is."

He led them down the cliff's base a bit to where a landslide had piled a jumble of boulders up against the wall. Kai started to climb with the mercenary Penny right behind him. Ayaan gave the boulders a look, adjusted his fanny pack to near the base of his spine, and followed. Marcus, Williams, and Destro joined the ascent.

Grant froze in place, staring at the pile.

"Problem?" Deborah said.

"No, other than falling down all those jagged rocks, or having someone kick one down on my head from up above, or having the whole pile collapse and grind me up like fruit in a blender. Other than those tiny issues, no problem."

Deborah pushed him aside. "What a wussy. You need to get out of your college campus bubble, Professor, and get out in the natural world."

"I get out in the natural world plenty," Grant said. "That's why it scares the crap out of me."

Deborah began to ascend the pile. Her shoe dislodged a golf ball-sized stone. It bounced once and hit Grant in the chest.

"Maybe it isn't any safer down here," Connor said.

"Doesn't look like it," Grant said.

"Just pretend you are that hero professor in your novels," Connor said. "He'd just run right up these rocks."

"That guy's an idiot," Grant said.

He began to pick his way up the pile with Connor behind him. Sonoma brought up the rear. Following in Deborah's footsteps, he quickly saw he wasn't going to keep up with her. The marathon running bitch was as nimble as a squirrel. Grant huffed and puffed with every step, regularly dropping to all fours in some spots for better balance. Deborah just hopped from rock to rock. Carrying a dozen extra pounds around his midsection definitely wasn't giving him an optimal center of gravity.

He was absolutely getting in shape if he lived through this experience. This time he was serious.

The group emerged on a flat, open space about twenty meters up from the forest floor. The steep sides all around meant no mammoths were going to climb up for a visit. A narrow overhang from the rock wall provided a little shelter. Under it opened a small cave that looked like it was only a meter or two deep. Sacks and boxes with Russian labels on the outside packed the cave.

"I thought you just had some protein bars?" Grant said.

"Initially, that was what I took with me," Kai said. "I snuck back in for supplies a few times since then."

"How long ago was the mammoth attack?" Destro said.

"Two weeks, maybe more. Kind of lost track of the days. Help yourselves to something."

The group descended on the cache. A box of protein bars was on top. Destro opened it, took one, and passed the box around.

The label was in Russian and the picture on the front clearly showed a delicious bar of nuts and chocolate chips drizzled in white yogurt. Grant grabbed a bar and tore open the wrapper. He took a bite and chewed. He almost spat it out.

The god-awful thing tasted like compressed sawdust. The bar inside the wrapper looked like particle board.

"As soon as I get home," Grant said, "this company is being sued for false advertising."

He hoped his assumption about getting home wasn't wishful thinking.

CHAPTER TWELVE

General Konstantine Vatutin beamed from the base of the cargo plane ramp. The Spetsnaz soldiers he'd borrowed from the Russian GRU surrounded the plane, weapons at the ready. Gavrie Popov stood to his left, ashen-faced and slumping.

Popov had been one of the haughtiest of the oligarchs, convinced he was omnipotent and untouchable, shielded by the wealth his empire of oil and natural gas fields generated. A few minutes at the hands of Vatutin's personal guard had cleared up that misconception. Vatutin had never seen the man look so defeated, and it made him smile.

"Sergeant Brusilov!" Vatutin barked.

A stout, rugged looking senior sergeant trotted up to Vatutin's side. A nasty burn on his scalp had left a patch of lumpy red scar tissue where hair had once been. "Yes, General."

"Secure the lab."

The sergeant nodded and set out with a squad of soldiers to the lab building. They charged through the front door.

Vatutin gave Popov a slap on the back. "Cheer up, Popov. Your work is about to serve the motherland."

"This was not what we agreed to," Popov said.

"You've always known that wolves do not keep agreements made with sheep," Vatutin said. "You just thought you were the wolf."

"That's been cleared up."

"What did you expect to happen when you told me you lost contact with this island?" Vatutin said.

"I told you that I could handle investigating what happened."

"You couldn't handle keeping whatever it was from happening, so my trust in your abilities has evaporated. I could not let my investment here be put at risk."

"The investment here is all mine," Popov said.

"Financially. But I've invested my reputation, which is much more valuable. And you had a very limited grasp of these creatures' potential, anyway."

"Are you kidding?" Popov said. "They are worth a fortune to zoos all over the world."

"See, limited vision," Vatutin said. "The military will breed these until we can release a herd in Alaska. They'll decimate the oil industry, overrun military bases. Environmentalists will cry about killing them. By the time American courts rule on anything, the damage will be done and mammoths will be spreading into Canada. Our military will be right behind them."

At the other side of the airstrip, the sergeant stepped back out of the door of the lab building. He shouted that the place was secure.

"Excellent," Vatutin said. "Let's go see how much your people have screwed this up."

Vatutin led Popov and two other soldiers across the airstrip. The second plane had parked to the right. Its lowered ramp exposed an interior converted to transport the mammoths with a set of built-in cages, like animal acts in circuses used to use. Inside, soldiers readied the cages and unpacked tranquilizing guns.

The men entered the lab building. Popov sighed at the chaos of the destroyed lab. As he took a closer look, he gasped at the liters of dried blood.

"When did you hear from them last?" Vatutin said.

"Two weeks ago. An emergency transmission. The fence was down. Mammoths were in the compound. After that, they did not respond to our calls."

"There aren't any dead mammoths in the compound. Looks like your scientists don't know how to put up a fight."

"They were unarmed except for some tranq guns. They wouldn't have been prepared for an attack."

"Lucky for you," Vatutin said, "my soldiers are. And more than that, ready to go on the offensive." Vatutin looked around the room. "How big are the mammoths?"

"Nine or ten meters tall."

"Then how could one get in here to make this mess?"

"It couldn't. Even calves more than a few weeks old would be too large to fit through the door. Something else did this."

"Something like?"

"Well, to be honest—"

Sgt. Brusilov shouted for Vatutin from a few tables over. Vatutin went to him. The sergeant threw a red backpack on top of the table. It had patches of several American National Parks sewn onto it. Vatutin cursed and turned to Popov.

"You said there were no Americans on your team."

"There aren't. A few Japanese and one Indian but no Americans, no one even with American ties. That is not one of my people's backpacks."

"Then someone else is here and they ransacked the lab."

Another soldier approached Vatutin. He had a don't-shoot-the-messenger look on his face.

"General," he said. "The servers are running, but there doesn't seem to be any data stored on them. The time stamp on the historian shows that it was last accessed just over an hour ago."

"Security is compromised," Vatutin said. "Who knew about this place, Popov?"

"No one, I swear!"

This was a bad turn of events. Vatutin had brought enough men to bring back the first mammoth, but not enough men to fan out into the valley on a search-and-destroy mission. But now they would have to do both.

"Our fighter escort saw no other planes in the area," Vatutin said. "That means the American thieves are still here, and they have the lab records. Sergeant Brusilov!"

The sergeant seemed to appear out of nowhere and came to attention. "Yes, General."

"Set up perimeter security. Have one team sweep the compound for intruders." He turned to Popov. "How did your people capture mammoths?"

Popov went to a map on the wall and pointed to the north side of the valley. "See those red boxes? Those are trap sites the team set and there's a truck with a winch to get any captured animals back to the airstrip."

"Sergeant," Vatutin said. "Have a second team find and prep the tranquilizer guns. Then have them check the sites on that map. We need to trap some mammoths."

There was no way off the island except the airstrip, so Vatutin was confident that the Americans weren't going anywhere. Once he had his prizes loaded for their flight home, he'd redirect his troops to a task they had more experience with than hunting hairy elephants. Hunting human beings.

CHAPTER THIRTEEN

Finding Kai and his treasure trove had lifted the group's spirits. Having something to eat and a safe place where they could breathe easy made a world of difference.

From the edge of what Kai called his stone tree fort, Williams kept a close watch on the compound through his binoculars. Penny and Sonoma squatted by him field cleaning the AK-47s.

The rest of the group sat back near Kai's stash of goods in the cave. Marcus seemed the most nervous of the bunch, definitely the furthest from his element. He sat with his back against a big rock, staring off at nothing. Of all the group, Grant felt most sorry for Marcus. He approached the anesthesiologist.

"You doing okay?" Grant said.

Marcus glanced around the area to be sure no one else was within earshot. "Honestly, I'm pretty scared."

"Woolly mammoths are scary."

"I'm not scared of those as much as I am of Destro. All the tranqs are in the valley. Destro has no need for me. What's to keep him from having one of those mercenaries kill me?"

"He's a scummy jackass, but he's no cold-blooded killer."

"Maybe not in a normal situation, but do you think this situation is normal?"

Grant had to admit that it wasn't. Even for him, with his history of being hunted by giant monsters.

"I'm not fearless," Marcus said, "like these mercenaries. I've spent a lifetime avoiding conflict, being introverted. I joke that I became an anesthesiologist so I didn't have to talk with my patients. I cheated on billing, something I've seen so many people do, and now I'm going to be shot to death near the North Pole."

Grant's heart went out to the poor guy, another person victimized and exploited by Destro. "Don't worry. The rest of us won't let that happen."

"Really?"

"Really. We all want to get home, and we all want everyone else to get home. Maybe Destro excepted."

Marcus managed a tiny smile. "Yeah, maybe if he got trampled by a mammoth, it would be okay."

Grant left Marcus to sort through his own thoughts. He pulled one of the sawdust bars from his pocket. He had rationalized that even if they had the nutritional value of dried celery, at least they made him feel full. Grant opened his third bar of the day. Some kind of worm crawled out of the center of the bar.

"I'm not that desperate for protein yet," Grant said.

He tossed the bar off the ledge and went over to where Kai sat with the group.

"Maybe you can shed some light on the mysteries of this place," Grant said.

"I've been keeping supply inventory for this team since the first day," Kai said. "I can't tell you about the science stuff, but I know how many rolls of toilet paper the group used each week."

Out of curiosity, Grant almost asked how many, then stopped himself.

"So," Grant said, "you were here when this place opened?"

"No, just with this team when it arrived. The compound had been built much earlier, but had obviously been abandoned long before we arrived. We unlocked the doors to a lab coated in dust and teeming with rust. There were computers so old they had floppy disc drives. None of them worked, but we'd brought all new tech."

"That explains the antiquated geothermal plant in the basement," Deborah said.

"The engineers with us called it 'mothballed', whatever that meant. It took them a few days to get it up and running. I thought going without a shower for those first days was roughing it." Kai looked around the barren rock ledge where they sat. "Now I have a much better idea of what 'roughing it' means."

"Why would Popov go to all this trouble earlier, and then abandon the compound?" Connor said.

"Maybe that first project failed," Grant said. "The kind of tech Kai describes is over twenty years old, even by Russian standards. Maybe the science of the time wasn't up to the task Popov assigned them."

Ayaan patted the fanny pack on a belt around his waist. "I've got the answer to that right here somewhere. Thumb drives full of everything on their server. Some of those file types were like completely archaic."

"I doubt they were trying to resurrect a mammoth that far back," Grant said. "There weren't even any good mammoth samples."

"That we know of," Destro said. "There's always something special floating around on the black market."

"You ought to know," Grant said.

"Sure, look down on me because I want to make a decent living digging up fossils, while you want to do it 'for science' and be so poor that you have to write monster books to feed yourself."

"Kaiju thrillers is the actual genre name," Connor corrected.

Grant rolled his eyes. "I don't write those to put food on the table. They are just for the satisfaction of entertaining people."

"When I entertain people," Destro said, "it's with a five-star dinner overlooking a beach somewhere. I move in circles you've never heard of."

"I've read Dante's *Inferno*. I'm well aware of the circles you move in."

"You have a big mouth for a guy who needs a ride home."

"You have a lot of optimism for a guy with Russian soldiers all over the runway his plane needs to use."

"Your plane is coming back?" Kai said.

Williams joined the group. "The pilot, Drew, promised to fly back in two days. But the sun doesn't set this far north this time of year, does it?"

"No," Kai said. "It screws with you after a while. You all need to force yourselves to get some sleep."

"Maybe the plane will rescue us before it gets to that," Marcus said.

"There's no way Drew tries to land with all those Russian planes on the field," Williams said.

"Does the plane need that whole runway?" Kai said.

"No, maybe half of it."

"Then there's another place it could land. The ridge at the top of the valley is flat and about that long. It's above the temperate line so it's Arctic summer up there."

"How summery is that?" Grant said.

"Right about freezing."

"Balmy. Glad I'm already in shorts."

"If we were up on the ridge," Williams said to Destro, "your radio would have better range."

Destro checked his pocket and pulled out the radio. "I could radio the pilot about the change in location before he even gets close to the airstrip."

"The Russians will never know he was here," Williams said.

"Or that we were, once we get on the plane," Destro said. "Let's get moving."

"Whoa!" Grant said. "Anyone remember that there are killer mammoths out in the woods?"

"You'd prefer to live the rest of your life here?" Deborah said.

"Let me see…a long life here or a short life after being sliced and diced by mammoths? Here sounds pretty good. After the Russians leave, we can go back to the compound and have the plane pick us up."

"There's no telling when the Russians will leave," Destro said.

"And I know our pilot," Williams said. "His loyalty is driven by a paycheck. The one trip back he promised is all we are going to get."

"Then up we go," Destro said.

Grant looked out over the carpet of pine trees that swept up the mountainside and into the mist. A herd of killer mammoths roamed under those branches. He hoped they didn't meet them.

CHAPTER FOURTEEN

Kai didn't have an actual map of the valley, but he drew a rough one to show the route to the rest of the group. He explained that it would be a long hike, first up to the lake that fed the stream that ran into the compound, then to the plateau beyond.

"Exploring the woods can be kind of dangerous," Kai said. "So I'll admit that I haven't been to all of these places, I just know of them."

"You've lived on this island for a while," Grant said. "One thing I don't get is what happens here in the winter."

"There's no winter," Deborah said. "The thermal energy keeps the place warm."

"But it doesn't keep it lit," Grant said. "Just as we aren't seeing a sunset now, in winter the place goes months without sunrise. How does all this survive without sunlight?"

"I do know that much of the science," Kai said, "since I witnessed it. The plant life goes black and dormant. Animal life hibernates until the sun comes back up."

"That's plausible," Grant said. "Especially if the ground never freezes because of the geothermal heat. If I live through this, I may write a paper on the idea."

"No one would publish it," Connor said. "Too far out there. You'll need to put it in your next novel."

"If this becomes a novel," Deborah said, "leave me out of the story."

"No worries," Grant said. "I like having the monsters be the most hated character and you might usurp that."

With the route planned out, the group packed for the trip, carrying as much food and water as they could. Kai passed out flashlights with strobes that might help the plane find them on the plateau. But Kai's cache was short on weapons or anything else to defend them from giant mammoths, so all they had were the AK-47s carried by the three mercenaries and Destro. Grant had seen the coat of the mammoths up close in the lab, and how ineffective rifle fire had been against it during the attack on the compound. But since the Russians weren't bulletproof, he guessed it was worth having the assault rifles at the ready for them.

After they climbed down from the perch on the granite, Connor went over to Kai.

"I guess you aren't going to miss this place," he said.

"Until I met all of you," Kai said, "I was afraid I was going to be trapped here until I died or a mammoth killed me. The sooner your plane gets us out of here, the happier I'll be."

The group headed out through the forest. Time was of the essence so Williams led them on a straight line through the trees with the help of his machete and a compass that seemed to stutter a lot due to the proximity of the North Pole. Grant was not filled with confidence.

After over an hour of uphill trekking, the breeze brought a whiff of something horribly unpleasant, disgustingly swampy and wholly unclean. The sensation passed, but a few minutes later, the smell returned, this time with a vengeance. Grant recognized it. That putrid stink always sent his stomach roiling. He knew the stench of a decaying carcass when it assaulted his nose.

"Ugh," Deborah said. "What the hell is that?"

"Something we'd rather not see," Grant said.

He'd come across many animal carcasses while working in the field. The more they reeked, the bigger they were. And this one was a stinker. The realization sent a shiver up his spine.

Up ahead, brighter daylight shined in the forest. The group entered a clearing. The rotting stumps of three dead trees in the center testified to how the open space had gotten its start. But the space had recently become unnaturally larger. All around the edge of the clearing, downed branches and broken tree limbs littered the ground. The earth had been churned up by the frenzied footwork of mammoths.

It appeared that one behemoth's struggle had been in vain. The rotting corpse of a woolly mammoth lay on its side across one of the downed trees. A gust of wind ruffled its hair and the armored strands clacked together like a bone windchime.

Williams sent the other two soldiers to the edges of the clearing.

The mammoth was about half the size of the one that had attacked the compound. The tusks that protruded from its upper lip were only a foot long and more rounded than sharp. The head was unmolested, save the hollowed-out eye sockets. The body was another story. The chest cavity had been torn open; the furry skin ripped apart on both sides like pages to an open book. White ribs poked out of the mess. The viscera remaining inside had decomposed into a black ooze.

Marcus held his nose and turned away. "Oh, that's disgusting."

Ayaan and Deborah took a few steps back to the far edge of the clearing. A slurping sound came from the mammoth's chest. Grant's gut instinct was to run, but as it annoyingly often did, the scientist in him demanded curiosity be satisfied. He stepped closer. The stench of the corpse became overwhelming. He held his nose and looked inside the creature.

The viscera ooze moved. A huge millipede crawled out of the mess. It was two centimeters wide and as long as Grant's forearm. It marched out of the corpse and toward Grant.

He jumped back. The millipede crawled away and disappeared under the bed of pine needles.

"What was that?" Deborah said.

"Those are new to me," Kai said.

"Looked like a giant millipede," Grant said. "They went extinct even before the mammoths did."

"And these sickos resurrected giant millipedes?" Marcus said.

"Maybe not," Grant said. "This isolated valley is like an island in the Pacific, just surrounded by ice instead of the sea. Whatever was here when the rest of the world changed could have survived, like these plants. Over centuries, things may have mutated to be even better adapted. Plenty of insects burrow in for winter and hibernate in the soil."

"So those things could be crawling around under our feet right now?" Marcus said.

"I'd say they definitely are. Something needs to aerate the soil to get these trees to grow."

"I wish I'd worn cleats," Marcus said.

"This totally needs to be in your next book," Connor said.

Destro was giving the head of the mammoth corpse a close inspection. He grabbed one tusk and gave it a shake.

"Any piece of this thing is worth a fortune," Destro said.

"But is it worth your life?" Grant said. "Elephants have a superior sense of smell plastered inside that long trunk. I wouldn't want the scent of a relative's blood on me if I happened upon a mammoth."

Destro dropped the tusk and checked his hands for any blood or hair.

"How did a millipede kill a mammoth?" Kai asked.

"It didn't," Grant said. "Look at how that skin is torn away, the strips of meat pulled from the ribs. Something else hunted this thing and killed it."

"Dammit," Williams said. "You're telling me there's something slinking around out here that can bring down a mammoth?"

"Yes," Grant said. "Congratulations. In this valley, you are not the apex predator. Humans might not even rate second place."

"Then let's get the hell out of here," Williams said. "The faster we get to that plateau landing area, the faster we are out of these woods."

Williams took the lead again with Kai behind him. They cut a path through the trees, but the going kept getting slower as the forest grew denser. They came across a larger trail that headed uphill. Big, round footprints covered the ground.

"Mammoth trail," Grant said. "Not the best route to use."

"But it goes uphill and it's clear," Williams said. "I'm not risking missing the plane. Let's use it."

"See that cairn, that pile of rocks," Kai said.

He pointed to a pyramid of rocks stacked up just off the trail. It obviously wasn't a natural formation.

"The scientists who went into the forest set those up to mark trails they used. Kept them from using maps or relying on compasses."

"There you go," Destro said. "Safe as a crosswalk in front of a police station."

Grant disagreed, but was in no position to argue with the man holding the gun. Kai headed up the trail and the group followed.

A few minutes later, fallen branches covered the trail. The pine needles on them had turned a sickly brown. A few yards farther down, a blackened object a half-meter wide and a meter long hung from a branch over the trail.

The others were too intent on scanning the woods for mammoths and the ground for millipedes that they did not seem to notice. As Grant got beneath it, he stopped.

"Hey, hold up,' he said.

The group paused.

The hanging object kind of looked like a fruit, but Grant knew pine trees of any species didn't fruit like this, and he hadn't seen something like this anywhere else. At about fifteen meters over his head, he couldn't make out any details.

"Williams," he said. "Can I borrow your binoculars?"

Williams stepped up behind him and passed him his field glasses. Grant put them to his glasses and focused on the fruit.

It sure wasn't fruit. It was a small cargo net, suspended from a rope. Whatever was inside the netting had accumulated a thick coating of moss.

"I'll be damned," Grant said.

The rest of the group closed in around him out of curiosity. Something creaked underneath his feet. He looked down at the pine bough he stood on. Desiccated needles fell from the branch, trickled down into the space between the branches, and disappeared.

"Hell, no," Grant said to himself. Then louder he said "Okay, everyone needs to—"

The ground underneath the group gave way and they tumbled down into darkness.

CHAPTER FIFTEEN

In Grant's mind, the one-second fall happened in agonizing slow motion and took forever. When he finally hit the ground, he was lucky that puffy pine boughs broke his fall. It still hurt like hell, but a quick check reassured him that nothing was broken.

"What do you know," he said to himself. "Still not dead."

Williams was up on his feet first. He began a frantic search for his AK-47 among the thicket of broken pine branches. The others slowly stirred, most with a moan.

They were at the bottom of a pit. The humid air smelled of peat and decayed plants. The pit's rectangular shape and the scraped earth sides betrayed that it wasn't natural. It had been dug out and then covered as a trap.

Williams recovered his weapon and gave it a quick inspection. He whooped with relief as he found it undamaged. He scanned the inside of the pit. His eyes stopped at the back.

Penny lay there with his head pulled back at an angle only turtles could survive. One of his splayed feet pointed in the opposite direction than it should have. Williams went to him, knelt down, and checked for a pulse. Then he swept a hand across the man's face to close his eyes.

Ayaan helped Marcus to his feet. The poor anesthesiologist looked almost catatonic from fear. Sonoma rose and pulled some branches off Deborah. She stood up and fluffed pine needles out of her hair. Connor sat up and scraped a swath of dirt from his lips. Destro used his rifle as a crutch to pull himself out of the boughs.

Williams muttered something to himself and stood back up. "Anyone else hurt?"

"No," Destro said, as if his own well-being was all that really mattered. He brushed some pine needles off his shirt. "Killer mammoths aren't enough? This valley is booby trapped as well? I'm lucky I wasn't killed."

"Fate certainly smiled on us with that one," Grant said.

"It wasn't luck," Deborah said. She parted some of the broken boughs to reveal that the entire floor of the trap was coated in cushioning pine. "If this trap was to kill us, there'd be something sharp down here. Instead, it was lined with something soft."

"Penny must have gotten caught on the edge," Williams said.

"They captured the baby mammoth in a trap like this," Kai said.

"And whatever's inside that mossy ball overhead was bait," Grant said. "And it worked."

"Why didn't it collapse when you first stepped on it?" Williams said.

"It had to support the weight of up to a baby mammoth until the animal got to the center."

"Still sounds like it should have collapsed when you first stepped on it," Deborah said.

"When we get home," Grant said, "I'm going to introduce you to my ex-wife. You two can start a coven."

"Both of you shut up and find a way out of here," Williams said.

"No need for that," came a voice from above.

Grant looked up to see the face of a Russian soldier staring down at him. Acne scars pocked his cheeks and his close-set beady eyes looked reptilian. Then three more soldiers appeared along the sides of the trap with rifles pointed at the group.

"This day just keeps getting better," Grant said.

"Drop the weapons," the lead soldier said to Williams.

Williams, Destro, and Sonoma tossed their AK-47s aside. A rope uncoiled as it dropped into the pit.

"That's a lot of people to drag up from that pit," one of the soldiers said.

"That's true," the lead soldier said.

He aimed his rifle at Sonoma and pulled the trigger. The blast echoed in the pit. Destro screamed.

The bullet hit Sonoma square in the chest. The impact threw him against the earth wall. He slumped down to the nest of pine boughs and didn't move.

"There you go," the soldier said. "One less to worry about. No need to bring back their guards."

He aimed his gun at Williams.

Suddenly, a black and tan blur rocketed across the top of the pit and swept the lead soldier out of view. A series of feline roars pierced the air. Another furry blur leapt across the opening at a different angle.

Grant dove for the ground. Whatever was going on up there he wanted to be as far away from it as possible. He burrowed into the pine branches.

Automatic weapons fire burped above. Big cat growls mingled with human screams. Undergrowth rustled as soldiers fled and hunting cats pursued. Then everything went quiet.

Grant looked up. A pine branch rolled off his head. The rest of the group was still standing. Deborah looked at him with disgust. His face went red.

"I slipped on some branches," he muttered. He stood up and pulled a pine branch out of the top of his shirt. Sap had glued itself to a few chest hairs and the strands came out at the roots. Grant winced.

Williams went to Sonoma's side. He checked for a pulse but the man's gray pallor said that was just a formality. Williams shook his head in anger. He sprang up and slung his rifle across his shoulders. He ran for the rope and jumped. The mercenary landed a third of the way up, caught the rope in both hands, and scaled it to the top. He jumped up on the edge of the pit and swung his rifle to the ready. He didn't fire.

"Oh my God," he whispered.

Williams stepped away out of view. Destro scooped his discarded rifle out of the branches. He pointed it at Grant.

"Someone needs to see what's going on up there," he said.

"Go ahead," Grant said. "I'll wait."

Destro jabbed Grant with the barrel. "After you. I insist."

Grant looked at the rope. Williams might have climbed it like a monkey, but no way Grant was going to have an easy time of it. But there wasn't any other way out of the pit. He went to the bottom of the rope. Connor came up beside him, knelt down and laced his fingers together.

"Let me get you started," he said.

Grant grabbed the rope and then tucked one foot into the kid's hands. Grant pulled himself up as Connor boosted him up. Then Grant planted both feet against the dirt wall and began a slow walk up the side. Arm muscles he wasn't even aware he had began to burn.

Hand over hand, step by step, he scaled the wall. With each motion, his pulse jumped up to a higher rate. Sweat beaded on his brow.

"I'd have already been up there by now," Deborah said from down below him.

"But you aren't as expendable," Destro said.

Grant didn't have the breath to tell Destro what a jerk he was.

He got to the edge of the pit and pulled himself over. He rolled on his back and took in a deep breath.

"Gym membership," he said. "Top of the to-do list when I get home."

He pulled himself to his feet and looked around. It looked like the soldiers had been spun out of a blender. Russian soldiers were torn to pieces all around the pit. So many arms and legs had been dismembered that Grant couldn't begin to count the number of casualties. Wide trails of blood across the forest floor indicated that some of the victims had been dragged away.

The forest was still. The predators had accomplished their mission and moved on.

"It's safe," Grant called down into the pit.

Williams stood over the carcass of a big cat. Grant picked his way around the gore to join him.

The cat was slightly larger than a full-grown tiger, with a tan coat spotted in black. The forelimbs were much more developed, the neck massively thick. It had to be to support the oversized skull and the two elongated canines that jutted down from the upper jaw.

"What the hell is this?" Williams said.

"It looks like a *Smilodon*," Grant said. "Commonly referred to as a saber-tooth tiger."

The rest of the group had each crawled up from the hole in half the time Grant had. They converged around the tiger.

"Wow," Connor said. "Is that a *Smilodon*?"

"Literally in the flesh," Grant said. He turned to Kai. "Were you going to mention these to us?"

"I didn't know these were out here. All anyone ever talked about were mammoths."

"*Smilodon*?" Ayaan said. "I remember some of the really old files had that in the title."

"And you weren't going to mention that?" Grant said.

"Like I'm supposed to know what that means. You asked for mammoth files."

"Kai, you said you weren't Popov's first group to work in the compound," Destro said. "Maybe this was what the first group was working on."

"Giant feline carnivores?" Grant said. "Then killer mammoths? Why doesn't anyone try and resurrect Pleistocene bunny rabbits? Am I the only person who's seen the *Jurassic Park* movies?"

"Why would the first team just pack up and leave these things roaming around?" Deborah said.

"When I asked about the previous group," Kai said, "I was told that the experiments failed and the work was abandoned."

"Maybe they thought everything they'd created had died," Connor said.

"Or maybe they made something so dangerous they were afraid to confront it and evacuated," Marcus said, "hoping that without prey, the cats would die off."

"Whatever their plan was," Grant said, "it left a pack of saber-tooth tigers roaming the valley. Maybe they lived off millipedes before mammoths. Those teeth could do a good job digging."

Destro knelt down and picked up one of the tiger's paws. He squeezed the center pad and a set of enormous, curved claws extended.

"Everything here is worth a fortune," he whispered.

"And it needs to stay here," Grant said. "Let's just get us out of here alive."

"Of course," Destro said.

Grant didn't believe him for a second.

CHAPTER SIXTEEN

General Vatutin paced the lab floor. He gave an empty cardboard box in the middle of the aisle a savage, frustrated kick. As his mistress always told him, he was not a patient man. He passed by Popov, who sat sulking on a stool in the corner of the lab.

"Cheer up, Popov," he said. "We will soon harvest the fruits of your labor."

"You'll harvest them," Popov said.

Vatutin stopped in front of Popov and stared down at him with a smile.

"What did you think would happen? How did you think this story would end? That I would provide you cover for your experiments and expect nothing in return? That somehow a little fish like you would swim with sharks and not get eaten?"

"We had a deal."

"Do you know what amuses me? Watching you oligarchs strut around and spend your money and think that you have power, that you are untouchable. There is only one source of power in the world." Vatutin slapped the holstered pistol at his side. "You are all just children squabbling on a playground. Eventually, the adults step in."

Behind Popov, a soldier worked at a laptop. Open computer file folders filled the screen. All of them were empty.

"Did you find anything on the computers to tell us what happened?" Vatutin said.

"Nothing, General," the soldier said. "Every file on the server is empty."

"There are security cameras," Popov said. "That video should tell us what happened here."

"Except all the camera footage is gone."

"Lost?" Vatutin said.

"Erased," the soldier answered, "the same as the research data. The entire main server had been stripped clean, and by someone who knows how to do it permanently."

"Goddamn Americans," Vatutin said. "If they get the research data back home, my plan loses the element of surprise and plausible Russian deniability."

The lab's front door swung open. Private Yurchik Laskin staggered in. The teenager's uniform was filthy, his ammunition pouches empty, and he carried no weapon. The fact that he was in the building, and not his squad leader, meant something was wrong. His disheveled condition meant the situation was catastrophic.

Vatutin strode over to the boy. He came to a weak version of attention and saluted.

"General, Private Laskin reporting."

"What is it, Private?"

"Sir, the squad was wiped out. I barely made it back. We found the Americans. They were trapped in a big pit."

Popov stepped up behind Vatutin. "The mammoth traps I showed you earlier. They must have fallen into one."

"And the Americans wiped out your squad?" Vatutin said.

"No, General. A pack of animals. Like lions with spots and huge teeth, like a walrus."

Popov's jaw dropped and he leaned against a lab table.

"Lions?" Vatutin said. "There aren't any lions here. Just mammoths."

"They survived," Popov said to himself.

"What survived?" Vatutin said.

"I started to tell you earlier, a way to explain the attack in this lab. Decades ago, there was another team, the first one to use this compound. We were experimenting with bringing back other species. It was a different process, using DNA and RNA extracted from fossilized bone marrow and mummified remains uncovered on an expedition in the Urals. One of the creatures was a *Smilodon*, a saber-toothed tiger. We would inject the DNA into fertilized lion eggs. The success rate was poor, the animals malformed. This was late 20th century and the science wasn't up to the task."

"So you quit?"

"A virulent flu strain broke out in the compound after a supply delivery. Many of the scientists died of pneumonia before I could get a medical evacuation plane in. With the project failing and some key players dead, I told them to destroy any living animals and close the shop. The returning scientists said that they had."

"Then they must have lied," Vatutin said, "because there's a pride of saber-toothed tigers roaming the woods."

"Maybe they let the living animals go free rather than kill what they had worked so hard to create. Maybe the animals escaped in the confusion. The scientists probably assumed they would all starve to death anyway, but against all odds, those cats survived."

"That gives us something else to take home," Vatutin said. "Something smaller. Good." He turned back to the private. "The Americans were killed as well?"

"No, General. They were in the pit. The tigers did not jump down there."

"How can my soldiers be unable to kill some unarmed civilians?" Vatutin said. "Now things are worse. This American team has the research and has seen living proof that it works. We can't let them escape and tell the world."

"How can they leave?" Popov said.

"The same way they got here, however the hell that was. Private, how many Americans were there?"

"I counted eight, but only a few were armed. The one in charge was tall, had a beard, and a scar under his right eye."

"Destro," Popov said. "That double-crossing bastard."

"You know him?" Vatutin said.

"Yes. Killing him would do the world a favor."

"I know people who would say the same about you." Vatutin turned back to the private. "Get cleaned up and resupplied. You are going to lead a team back to that site. We're going on a lion hunt."

CHAPTER SEVENTEEN

Marcus broke the silence as the overwhelmed group stood amidst the carnage around the mammoth trap.

"You know, it was bad enough dealing with killer mammoths," he said. "Now we can toss being hunted by Russian soldiers and becoming prey for saber-tooth tigers into our anxiety backpacks."

"Into what?" Ayaan said.

"Anxiety backpack. A concept my therapist told me about. It represents how we burden ourselves with unjustified worry."

"I think all our worries are justified this time around," Connor said.

"This whole nightmare is the most terrifying thing I've ever experienced," Marcus said.

Grant thought back over his adventures the past few years. Even he had to agree with Marcus.

"What if those tigers are stalking us right now?" Marcus said.

"They aren't," Grant said. "Big cats either feed where they kill, or drag their prey back to a safe place they frequently use. Except for some stray severed limbs, this pride took the soldiers elsewhere."

"None of this changes that the clock is still ticking down until the plane arrives," Destro said. "We need to get moving again. We know the saber-tooths are out there and we can be ready for them."

A Russian's AK-47 lay on the ground half-covered in pine needles. Connor bent down and grabbed the barrel.

"Stop right there," Destro said.

Connor froze in place and looked up in confusion. "We might get attacked by those tigers again."

"And Williams and I will hold them off."

"Are you kidding?" Grant said. "There are abandoned guns lying around and we're not picking them up?"

"Let's just say I have trust issues," Destro said.

"As well you should," Grant said, "being a professional slimeball. But at this point, we're all in this together."

"Not really. I think that some of you, especially you, Grant, would be happy to see me dead."

"Of course, who wouldn't? But I can wait until we're somewhere south of the Arctic Sea."

"I'm committed to making sure you have to wait far longer than that," Destro said. "And keeping you disarmed makes that so much easier."

Grant looked over at Williams. He hoped that the mercenary would have a more reasonable opinion, one where the more guns the merrier when you were wedged between a pride of saber-tooth tigers and a herd of killer mammoths.

"Williams?" Grant pleaded.

Williams shrugged. "I side with the man who pays me, and, more importantly, who pays the pilot who will get us the hell out of here. And in my experience, firearms in untrained hands are worse than useless, they're dangerous."

"And so the rest of you know," Destro said, "if I don't make it back, I've left instructions to expose all our sordid business dealings to the world, and you'll be ruined. So it's in all your best interests that I stay alive. Now with that settled, let's get hiking."

Williams took the lead, and they continued up the trail. After a few kilometers it curved away from the direction of the plateau. Williams shot an azimuth with his compass and they struck out into the woods.

Soon the trees thinned a bit and then the group stood at the edge of a clearing. The wind had created drifts of pine needles that covered the space. Many of the drifts were over two meters high.

"What's this?" Grant asked Kai.

"No clue," Kai said. "I haven't been to this part of the valley before."

No one moved. Destro poked Grant with his rifle barrel. "What are you waiting for?"

"Looks kind of exposed," Grant said. "I was going to bring up the rear, check for stragglers."

"You get to go first, Mammoth Bait."

"Why do I keep going first?"

Destro jabbed Grant harder with the rifle. "Because I don't like you."

Grant made his way alone across the clearing. As he scanned the circle of trees around him, he was uncomfortably reminded of Christians being fed to lions in the Roman Colosseum. He stepped up his pace.

Halfway across, he rounded one of the mounds of needles and noticed something bright white sticking out of the drift. The scientific curiosity that regularly tried to get him killed kicked in. He stopped and brushed at the pine needles. They cascaded away to reveal a large dome of alabaster bone.

"What are you doing?" Destro shouted from the trees.

Grant bent down and dug at the base of the drift. An avalanche of needles fell away and buried his feet. The skull of a mammoth lay before him. It was likely from a younger one, based on the size and the relatively short tusks.

Grant went to the next drift. He swatted away some needles and exposed the tip of an upturned bone. He grabbed it with both hands and shook it. The drift sifted down to ground level and Grant had a grip on the lower rib of a full mammoth rib cage. He looked around and realized that he could see bones poking out of several other drifts.

The rest of the group left the forest and caught up with him. Destro took a look at the exposed skull and sucked in a deep breath. Deborah looked back and forth between the skull and the ribcage.

"Damn," Deborah said, "what happened here?"

"If all these drifts cover different skeletons," Grant said, "this is a lot of dead mammoths."

"Cool," Connor said. "This is the mammoth equivalent of an elephant graveyard."

"Elephants bury their dead?" Marcus said

"No," Grant said. "Supposedly there are places where the elephants go when they know they are going to die."

"I thought those were myths," Ayaan said.

"They are," Grant said. "At least for elephants."

Destro knelt beside the skull, and ran a finger along the tusk. "The tusks alone in this clearing would be worth a million dollars. I wouldn't even need to bring back live animals to turn a profit."

"There are dozens of drifts in this clearing," Grant said. "And I don't know about mammoths, but elephants live a long time. This has been going on a while. But for an animal to consciously know it is dying, and still have the energy to get here? That seems like a stretch."

Then he thought about the skull at his feet. That wasn't from some aging mammoth ready to cash in its chips. And these skeletons were still fully articulated. Saber-tooths should have scavenged the corpses as free meals and torn the carcasses apart.

The whole thing didn't make sense. One of his favorite rules of paleontology was that if all the data didn't support your first hypothesis, then there was a damn good chance that first hypothesis was wrong.

He caught a whiff of rotten eggs. He kicked the pine needles away from the ground at the base of the skull. A centimeter-wide crack ran across the hardened ground. The edges were tinted in yellow and orange. His jaw dropped. He turned to the group.

"Everyone run!" he shouted. "Before we all die!"

CHAPTER EIGHTEEN

The data did support Grant's second hypothesis, and that hypothesis was terrifying. All the mammoths around Grant had been killed by breathing CO_2 leeching out of the ground, and humans weren't immune.

The panic in Grant's voice must have convinced Williams that he could wait for an explanation. "Go, go, go!" he shouted and then he took off for the tree line.

Destro stared at Grant with a questioning look, as if uncertain whether Grant was being serious or sarcastic. The others scattered and ran for the trees in different directions. Grant kicked at the crack in the ground.

"CO_2 gas! You'll suffocate."

Grant wasn't going to let saving Destro's evil life keep him from saving his own. The man could stay if he wanted to. Grant bolted for the edge of the clearing. Destro seemed to put the story together in his head and then began to sprint.

Grant followed in Williams' tracks. To say that running wasn't his forte would be a horrific understatement. He made for the woods in an adrenaline-fueled rush. Leg muscles caught fire as he stretched them to their limits. His stomach bounced up and rolled over his belt with each pounding step. Every gasping breath he took seemed to sear his lungs, and he wondered if that was psychological or if he was indeed poisoning himself faster with his rapid-fire panting.

Williams made it to the clearing's grassy edge and stopped. Grant crossed that same finish line completely out of breath. He dropped to his knees.

Out in the clearing, Marcus cried out. He poked out of the ground between two pine needle drifts. The earth beneath him had collapsed and swallowed his legs up to the knee. His face glowed bright red as he tried and failed to lever himself out of the hole with his arms.

Grant's stomach sank. A geological site seeping geothermal vapors was also prone to gas pockets under weak crust. Marcus had broken through to one of those pockets. The rapid release of the stored CO_2, and his proximity to the ground, meant he wouldn't last long.

Grant rose to his feet with sweat pouring down his face. He was the last person in the world to be heroic, but he couldn't deny Marcus' pleading eyes and plaintive cry. He moved to return to the clearing.

Williams clamped a hand on Grant's shoulder and pulled him back. Grant was honestly too out of breath to resist.

"Too late," Williams said. "It will just kill you as well."

Marcus' face went ash white and his eyes bulged. Both hands went to his neck as his mouth gaped open and closed like a fish out of water. His eyes rolled up in his head and he fell face-first into the pine needles. With one more shuddering heave, his chest collapsed and then he went still.

Grant dropped back to his knees physically, and now emotionally, drained. Penny and Sonoma were mercenaries who'd chosen these risks, players in a game they knew might deal them the bad cards they'd drawn. But Marcus...the poor man didn't need to be here, didn't need to face all these dangers. How could this be explained to his family?

The rest of the group made their way around the clearing's perimeter and formed up on Williams.

"Where's Marcus?" Ayaan said.

Williams pointed to Marcus' body. "Didn't make it."

Ayaan's face fell. "Aw, I was starting to like the dude."

"What the hell was that out there?" Deborah said.

"Release of CO_2 gas is common in geologically active areas like this," Grant said. "It will kill the roots of anything growing there, and then overcome any passing animals if the concentration is high enough. It's odorless, but I smelled the sulfur it carried with it and saw fissures in the ground stained with airborne minerals."

"The mammoths didn't come here to die," Connor said. "They came here *and* died."

"Exactly."

"And we all almost joined them," Ayaan said. "What can we do for Marcus?"

"Nothing," Destro said. "We keep moving. The Russians will come looking for that patrol the saber-tooths slaughtered."

Grant saw Connor look hurt by Destro's callous response. Grant tried to soften it. "If we go out there to try and get his body, we could all end up just as dead."

Destro waved his rifle at the group. "Get a move on. We have a plane to catch."

CHAPTER NINETEEN

The group trudged on for over an hour. A lack of sleep and a lack of darkness had Grant feeling fuzzy. It reminded him of staying up all night studying for finals, except that he had done that with the stamina of a nineteen-year-old. Williams must have sensed the rest of the group felt the same. The mercenary called a halt.

"What are you doing?" Destro said.

"Keeping people from dropping dead. Ten-minute break."

Everyone hit the ground. Even Deborah looked a bit taxed. That made Grant happy.

As they took a snack break of sawdust bars, Williams went down the line and handed everyone two packets of instant coffee.

"You putting on a kettle?" Grant asked. "I do cream and two sugars. I'll take mine in the drawing room, please."

"You all need to stay alert," Williams barked at the group. "This is the strongest thing we have to help with that. Rip it open, pour it in your mouth, and wash it down. Tastes like hell, probably will upset your stomach, but the caffeine will hit you hard."

Most in the group looked sideways at the packet in their hands.

Ayaan shrugged. "I've done so much worse than this."

He ripped open the packets, poured the contents into his mouth, and followed it with a big swig of bottled water. He winced and groaned.

"Okay," Ayaan said. "Maybe not much worse."

The rest followed Williams' instructions with similar reactions. Grant shredded his packets and tossed the coffee in his mouth. He washed it down and it felt like he was swallowing coffee grounds. It took a second swig to rinse leftover grains stuck on his teeth.

Seconds later acid swirled in his stomach. His body had no interest in percolating instant coffee at 98 degrees. He swallowed some more water but that seemed to make it worse.

Connor spat a few grains of coffee out of his mouth. "Wow, that was awful."

"At least we didn't wait in line with hipsters to get it," Grant said.

And then Grant was awake. Two grandes worth of Starbucks awake. Williams knew his stuff.

Williams called everyone to their feet. Grant practically jumped up. Williams led the group out with Destro last in line.

A half hour later, the trees thinned out. Then they came upon a clearing, half the size of the mammoth graveyard. Golden grass about knee-high carpeted the ground. A narrow path across the area had been beaten flat. Williams stopped and motioned Grant forward. Kai followed Grant.

"You think this ground will kill us?" Williams said.

"No guarantees anything on this island won't kill us," Grant said. "But all that grass is alive, so it's probably safe."

Destro apparently couldn't stand the suspense and joined the group of three.

"But mammoths didn't make that little trail down the middle," Grant added.

"My people did," Kai said. He pointed to a little pile of stones beside the trail.

"The path is heading in the right direction," Williams said.

"Follow it," Destro said to Williams.

Williams didn't look sanguine about entering the more open area, but he nodded and set out along the path. Grant was right behind him.

"Thanks for the break back there," Grant said. "And for not just charging across this clearing."

"I want to live through this," Williams said. "And believe it or not, I also want as many of you to do that as possible."

Grant's opinion of the mercenary started a slow shift to positive.

Halfway across, Connor shook his head and wrinkled his nose.

"This place smells awful," Connor said.

Indeed it did. But not sulfurous like the mammoth killing field. This scent was coppery, musky, with more than a whiff of ammonia.

"Damn," Deborah said. She turned her head away from the left side of the trail without breaking stride. "Check that out."

A shredded lab coat lay wadded in a pile off the trail. The dried blood on it had turned almost black. From the looks of it, the coat had been out here a while.

Then something worse appeared on the right side of the trail.

The severed arm of a Russian soldier lay in the grass. The uniform sleeve covered the arm from the elbow down, but the bicep had been reduced to a gnawed, grisly pulp. The snowy ball at the top of the upper arm bone shined a very bright white. Decay hadn't set in yet.

Grant's stomach took a churn as he looked at the grisly remains.

That had to be from one of the soldiers who were attacked at the pit trap, he thought. *But this was quite a way from there. How could this arm—*

A sound like a lion's chuff cut off his train of thought. Then two yards from the path, a saber-tooth tiger's head rose over the waving shafts of grass. It stared at Grant. Its eyelids looked heavy, and the big cat yawned.

The group froze. Destro stopped right behind Grant. He let out a curse and raised his rifle to blast the cat.

"No!" Grant whispered as he pressed the gun's barrel down.

Saber-tooth tiger heads rose from the grasses along both sides of the path. They'd walked into the center of the napping pride.

"I've seen this happen with African lions," Grant said. "These cats are fat and sleepy now, full of borscht-fed Russians. If they aren't hungry, and we aren't a threat, they'll just let us pass."

"Are you serious?" Deborah said.

"I've seen antelope saunter through a pride on a hot summer's day. Just keep going."

Williams began down the trail taking slow, deliberate steps. The rest of the group followed at the same pace. Grant had his head on a swivel, watching the droopy faces of the cats, looking for the hunting instinct to light up in one's eyes. Instead, they looked bored as house cats.

Suddenly, shouts in Russian came from the downslope clearing's edge. A squad of soldiers stepped out of the trees and into the grass. One of them pointed at Grant's group. A second soldier raised his rifle and sent a spray of poorly aimed rounds in Grant's direction.

The group ducked down into the grass.

The entire pride went to high alert. The tigers jumped to their feet as one. Every head locked on the Russian squad. The largest tiger, in the center of the pride, let loose a roar so deep Grant felt his organs vibrate.

Another soldier opened fire. Bullets clipped the tops of the grass. One round struck a tiger. Blood splashed everywhere. The big cat cried out with a shrieking roar and dropped onto the ground.

The pride roared in fury. The leader sprang from his position and charged the Russians. The pride sprinted in pursuit.

For such muscular, hulking cats, they ran astoundingly fast. The big cats sliced through the grass, showing only the top half of their heads and an occasional surfacing of their great shoulders. The smaller tigers bounded up and out of the grass like flying fish at sea to keep sight of their targets. Lines of crushed grasses pushed forward through the field, converging on the Russians.

The squad of Russians at the pit trap had been ambushed and unprepared. This new squad was not. The Russians opened fire. A hailstorm of bullets swept the grass. Tigers roared and wailed as hot lead found its targets. Several members of the pride dropped, but the rest kept sprinting. A tiger tackled the soldier closest to the charging pack. They disappeared into the grass and a fountain of blood sprayed into the air.

Two soldiers ran forward carrying rifle-propelled grenade launchers. They took a knee, aimed at the leader of the pride, and fired. The grenades boomed, but instead of sailing in and exploding, these inert warheads pulled trails of wire. The big cat launched itself into the air. The projectiles bracketed the saber-tooth.

The wires pulled a sheet of netting up off the ground. The pouncing tiger hit the net full force. The mesh wrapped around him like a shroud. The tiger hit the ground. Rolling in snarling fury, the restraint wrapped even tighter.

Gunfire continued on either side of the ensnared leader. Rounds ripped through fur and tigers died in agonized spasms of pain. Tigers at the rear of the attack pulled up short, looking confused at the loss of their leader and the dying cats in the grass. Grant thought they'd never been anything but the kings of the forest, and this was hard for them to process. Tigers broke for the trees in all directions.

With the attack repelled, all the soldiers swarmed to the captured tiger. They pulled the net tighter until the flailing saber-tooth was compressed into a ball. Deeper in the forest, a diesel engine rumbled to life.

"They were here to capture a saber-tooth," Williams said. "We were just a target of opportunity. Stay low and let's go while they're busy."

"Agreed," Destro said.

Williams began a crouching run to the tree line. The rest followed. Russian orders sounded from the soldiers, but it wasn't the sound of men preparing for a pursuit. They were engrossed with capturing the tiger without getting shredded. Williams didn't stop until the group was out of sight of the saber-tooth battlefield.

Grant collapsed to the ground. "You know what's funny? On my list of ways I don't want to be killed, shot by Russians and eaten by saber-tooth tigers are both near the top."

"The remaining cats will have a little fear of man in them now," Destro said, "and give us a wider berth."

"And the pride will have to reorganize itself around a new alpha," Grant said. "But that might not take long. And seeing man as a threat might make them more aggressive, not less."

"Even worse," Kai said. "The Russians saw us. That means they know you are here."

"We know why the Russians are here for sure," Deborah said. "They're bringing back specimens."

"And they won't want us left behind alive to tell the world about it," Grant said.

CHAPTER TWENTY

Once they had traveled far enough that the sounds of the Russians and their departing truck disappeared, the group took a break. Williams stopped them on a flat section of ground on the valley's steep side. While they rested, Connor went over to the edge facing the valley. His face paled.

"Uh, Grant?" he said. "Everyone? You might want to see this."

Grant followed the group to where Connor stood. Peering between the trees, they could get a good view of the valley below. Williams took out his binoculars for a closer look.

The mammoths had made a clearing in the forest. They'd pushed down trees, roots and all, and stacked them into a fence line around the perimeter. One mammoth-sized gap remained like an open gate. Craters in the clearing marked where the ball of roots of each tree had been ripped out, with one larger crater near the center.

The mammoths stomped and snorted as they paced the clearing. The largest one stood at the perimeter with its trunk wrapped around a tree trunk. The mammoth smashed it up and down against the perimeter wall.

The herd was larger than Grant had expected, and the age distribution much greater. There were many younger calves in the group. The calves already had tusks consistent with their size. The young ones aggressively sparred with each other.

"This behavior is all wrong," Grant said, "at least using elephants as a guide."

"What do you mean?" Deborah said.

"First, it looks like they built a corral. Downing trees like that by pushing them over is normal, but building a defensive barricade isn't. Elephants are smart, but not that smart."

"Maybe they just pushed them away and it only looks like they built something," Destro said.

"No," Deborah said. "The way those trunks interlock? That's engineered. They made this. Grant is right."

"I must not have heard you correctly," Grant said with feigned confusion. "Can you say that last sentence again?"

"Probably not. It seared my throat saying it once."

"Second," Grant continued, "there are way too many youngsters of all ages. African elephants have a gestation period of almost two years with an overall reproduction cycle of four to five years. The young in this herd are not five years apart. These mammoths are reproducing at a much faster rate."

"Since the herd goes into hibernation in the winter," Kai said, "maybe the young need to grow up quicker."

"Third," Grant said, "these things are pissed. Young elephants play, these mammoth calves are in mock combat. The entire herd is agitated and aggressive. It's like they are all in permanent musth."

"Musth?" Deborah said.

"A time when hormones flood male elephants' systems. They get hyper aggressive. This whole group, even the females, seems to be on a hormone high."

The mammoth that had been pounding a tree trunk stopped and stomped over to the larger pit in the clearing's center. It raised its trunk and trumpeted at the sky. The other mammoths stepped back from the crater and faced the leader.

The creature reached down into the pit with its trunk. The end disappeared beneath the lip of the hole. When it came back up, it was coiled around a human being. The terrified woman wore filthy, ragged clothes and her dark hair was matted and messy. She screamed as the mammoth lifted her over its head.

"That's Dr. Chen from the lab," Kai gasped.

The mammoth dropped her to the ground. She hit hard and rolled over on her back.

The creature bent its head down and laid the sharpened edge of one tusk against Chen's right leg. With an unbelievable level of precision, the mammoth flicked its head, and slashed the woman's leg. She shrieked and gripped the gash in her thigh with both hands.

The mammoth laid the opposite tusk against her left arm. Before the woman could react, the mammoth ripped open her bicep. Blood splashed along the tusk. The woman wailed as her wounded arm went flaccid. She collapsed to the ground, screaming with the shrieks of one gone insane with terror.

The matriarch's trunk curled around Chen, picked her up again, and then slammed her back on the ground. The woman's screams ceased. Her body went limp. The mammoth raised the corpse back up, and passed it to the mammoth on its right. The other mammoth trumpeted, then accepted the body. The second mammoth slapped the corpse against the ground as the leader had done.

The process continued around the crater as each mammoth passed the dead scientist to the next mammoth, who then smacked it against the ground. The battered body finally made it back to the leader. The leader bellowed loud enough to make the nearest tree branches sway, then took the dead woman in its trunk. It went to the perimeter's edge and stuck the body atop the tree trunk barrier. Then it lifted the tree that it had been pounding earlier and dropped it on the corpse, making it a macabre kind of mortar in the wall.

"Good God," Grant whispered.

"That doctor isn't the only victim," Williams said. He took his binoculars from his eyes and passed them to Grant.

Grant looked through the binoculars and focused on the top of the wall. Two dozen dead bodies stuck from the upper edge all along the perimeter. It looked like this ritual had been played out with team members from the compound. He passed the glasses to Kai.

"Oh no," Kai said as he looked at the wall. "So many of my friends."

"Mammoths took the people they caught inside the compound," Williams said, "and saber-tooths finished off the ones who took shelter in the lab."

"These mammoths are clearly intelligent," Grant said, "highly social, and fully psychopathic. Destro, you still want to try to bring one of those home?"

"I'm not getting anywhere near one," Destro said.

"These would be an ecological disaster if they were brought back and accidentally reintroduced," Grant said. "They'd slaughter other creatures, propagate quickly, and be difficult to kill without a huge amount of collateral damage."

"Can't that happen even without someone bringing them back?" Ayaan said.

"What do you mean?"

"Dude, they're woolly mammoths," he said. "Can't they wander out of this little Eden and walk across the frozen ocean to Asia and North America? They have fur coats for the snow."

Grant's gut sank. "Hell, you're right. Once the population exceeds what this valley can sustain, they will migrate, just like elephants do. The world won't be ready for that."

"That sounds like the world's problem," Destro said. "All I care about is getting out of here alive."

Grant had to agree that getting out of here alive was his top priority. But he wasn't going to ignore the two other things that had to be done: the Russians had to be stopped, and this whole experiment needed to be shut down and erased.

He had no idea how to complete the last two tasks.

CHAPTER TWENTY-ONE

Ayaan crept back to where the rest of the group was sleeping. Williams had called for a four-hour break to force everyone to rest during this endless Arctic day. Ayaan hadn't needed it. He had other plans.

None of this little excursion had been what Destro had promised. The dude had recruited him to do some ultra-simple hacking and to vacuum some files out of a server. "In and out" had been the phrase Destro used. That promise hadn't been fulfilled, unless you wanted to interpret the phrase as a metaphor for being screwed, and then the man had been dead-on truthful.

After the mammoth attack and the Russians' arrival, heading into the forest with Destro seemed like the best, maybe the only, viable option. The dude owed him money, plus, he was the transportation in, so he was going to be the transportation out, right?

But after seeing the mammoth compound, Ayaan had figured out that Destro didn't have it together. He was pretending he was in control of things, but that was a load of crap. Ayaan had known too many fakers to not spot one when the man stood right in front of him. Destro wasn't sure what creatures he was up against in the hills, was no match for the Russians in the valley, and was counting on an unseen plateau being long enough to land a hoped-for rescue plane. Ayaan had to admit he'd bet on the wrong team.

So now it was time to correct that mistake. He didn't owe Destro anything, and he had no particular beef with the Russians. The Russians had way more guns and a way to get the hell off this island. So, from a completely practical perspective, mid-stream or not, it was time to change horses.

And in case the Russkies were less than amenable to adding a new partner, he was going to arrive bearing gifts. All the thumb drives he'd filled with Popov's mad science stuff were in his fanny pack, liberated from Destro's undeserving ownership as he slept. Ayaan envisioned himself being accepted with open arms and celebratory shots of vodka. The Russians were big international hackers. He could even see this turning into an excellent career move.

He'd just relieved himself and now tiptoed back through the sleeping bodies of the rest of the team. It came to him that now was as good a time as any to sneak away. He could leave with no one knowing, and the longer he put it off, the further from the valley he'd be. He stopped where he'd been resting and reached to the ground for his fanny pack.

"What are you doing?" Connor whispered.

Ayaan's heart skipped a beat. He snatched the pack off the ground and clicked it around his waist.

So, everyone wasn't asleep after all, he thought.

"I'm taking off," Ayaan said. "These losers are all saber-tooth food, mammoth toys, or worse. Time to bail." Then he figured he might as well have company. "You in?"

"Where are you going?"

"Back to the place with an airstrip and a guaranteed way home. I'm too young and handsome to die out here."

"Saber-tooths will get you. Stay. Grant and the others will get us rescued."

"Dude, all these people will get you is turned into a predator entrée. Don't follow your professor into a saber-tooth's food bowl."

"Safety in numbers, bro. I'm sticking here."

"Suit yourself," Ayaan said. "Don't rat me out, okay?"

"Live and let live. Your life, your choice."

"Righteous. Later."

Ayaan picked his way through the group and back to the trail they arrived on. He waited a moment. The little camp stayed quiet.

Connor isn't ratting me out, he thought. *Excellent. Dude should have come along. When he's getting slashed in two by a mammoth, he'll wish he'd taken the offer.*

#

The view from Grant's beach chair looked like an ad for a travel company. Whitecaps tipped deep blue waves as they rolled in from the vast Pacific. Puffy, bright clouds dotted a pale blue sky. Waves crested and crashed offshore and their remnants surged in to kiss the white Hawaiian beach. The sun shined down rejuvenating rays and warmed Grant to his core.

A waiter in black pants and a white shirt crossed the sand and stopped at a small table to the right of Grant's chair. He set down a tray covered with a silver dome upon the table.

"Lunch is served," he said.

He pulled the cover away with a flourish to reveal the mother of all cheeseburgers. A patty the size of Grant's hand hung over the edges of a golden sourdough bun. Two colors of melted cheese drizzled down the patty's sides. Pieces of crisp bacon held the top bun suspended just off the patty to expose a swirl of ketchup and mustard. Beside the plate, a frosted glass of sparkling gold beer begged to quench Grant's thirst.

Grant's mouth watered and his stomach rumbled a demand to be filled. He reached for the burger. Something poked him hard in the side.

Grant awakened lying on the rocky ground overlooking the mammoth corral on Mammoth Island. The disappointment at not being in Hawaii was overwhelmed by the disappointment of not getting at that cheeseburger. His stomach growled its discontent at the teasing. The sharp prod to his side recurred. He rolled over on his back. Deborah stood beside him with a long stick in her hand.

"Rise and shine, Michelin Man," Deborah said.

"It's you," Grant said. "I was hoping to be awakened by something more pleasant, like a saber-tooth."

"No one will complain if you opt to stay here and meet one today. Be my guest."

The four-hour rest break seemed like it had lasted about fifteen minutes. But it was certainly better than nothing. Once they'd stopped on the outcrop that overlooked the corral, Grant honestly wasn't sure he could start hiking again without at least a little sleep.

Grant rose to his feet. Every joint seemed to creak and his back felt mangled from sleeping on cold, hard rocks. The rest of the group milled about. He didn't see Ayaan. Grant went over to Destro, who stood by a tree with a packet of instant coffee in one hand and a water bottle in the other.

"Where's Ayaan?" Grant said.

"Gone," Destro said. "Sometime while we were asleep. Saber-tooth might have grabbed him. Maybe he struck out for the plateau on his own. IT guys are all so squirrelly."

Destro tore open the packet and poured the coffee in his mouth, followed by a swig of water. He grimaced and shivered as he swallowed it down.

"We need to find him," Grant said.

"No, we don't," Destro said. "I had him give me the data files he downloaded, and I'm pretty sure we won't need any tech skills to get through this forest. Just another person to drain resources and slow us down."

"Damn, even you can't be that cold," Grant said.

"I've survived a long time doing business in dangerous places. I've learned how to maximize my survival odds with three rules. Be the highest bidder, hire ruthless people, minimize your risk. Chasing down Ayaan doesn't work in my favor. He's already given me everything I needed from him."

Destro patted the side pocket of his cargo pants with a smile. His look turned grim. He slapped his pants again, then shoved a hand in the pocket. It came back out empty.

"Lose something?" Grant said.

"That son of a bitch," Destro said. "He took all the flash drives."

"Maybe you weren't the highest bidder after all," Grant said.

#

Ayaan backtracked down the trail the group had ascended the day before. He'd skirt the spot where they'd encountered the tigers, and stay well clear of the mammoth graveyard. He wasn't an outdoorsman by any definition of the term, but he wasn't worried about getting lost. Even if he missed the specific path they'd been on, as long as he kept going downhill, he'd end up in the valley, and as long as he ended up in the valley, he could find his way back to the compound.

He snapped out of his daydream and realized, while he was still on some kind of path, it wasn't one the group had used going uphill. But it was still going down, so he convinced himself he was headed in the right direction. Generally.

He came to a steeper part of the trail. He half-skidded down the slick earth, using trees along the side for support as he passed them. At the bottom, the trail curved left and hugged a cliff face.

He slid to a stop at the curve, and looked up the trail. An AK-47 sat on the path propped up against the cliff. The banana-shaped magazine curved out from the weapon and even in the hazy sunlight the polished wood along the barrel twinkled.

Ayaan smiled at his stroke of good luck. One of the Russian soldiers on patrol must have left it behind. Ayaan was going to feel a hell of a lot safer wandering around out here if he could shoot anything big and hairy that lumbered onto the trail.

Of course, he'd never actually shot a rifle before. But how hard could it be? And all the animals out here were pretty damn big. How much aiming would he need to do?

He continued down the trail and stopped at the base of the cliff. He picked up the rifle. It was much heavier than he'd imagined. He turned it over in his hands. Hard to believe that the person who'd taken such good care of it had left it behind. Oh well. Losers, weepers.

Ayaan liked the feel of the gun in his hands. The Bollywood action-movie bad guys he'd grown up watching in India all carried AKs. He smirked and aimed the gun at some trees, butt stock against his hip, the way all movie bad-asses did.

A pebble dropped from the cliff and bounced off his shoulder. Something huffed from far above.

Ayaan looked up to see a mammoth's head leaning out over the edge of the cliff. Its trunk curled around a massive log, suspended over the trail. Ayaan could swear that he saw glee in its eyes.

Ayaan froze.

Had this elephant actually set a trap? Understood that a rifle would be good bait, and then waited for a human to happen upon it?

His stunned disbelief turned into terror as the mammoth's trunk relaxed and sent the tree trunk spinning down.

He wasted a split second realizing the log was hurtling toward him. He wasted another trying to decide which way to run. When he finally broke right to escape, it was too late. He got in two steps and looked up.

The next few milliseconds unwound in slow motion. The tree trunk took up more and more of his field of view until it blocked all the daylight and he could make out the grain pattern in the bark. He turned back to see the trail just as the trunk landed on his head.

The world returned to normal speed. The trunk's impact drove him hard and embedded him into the earth. Then the log bounced up and rolled off downhill.

Everything in Ayaan's body felt broken. Back, ribs, skull, feet. His crushed lungs couldn't draw a breath and he choked as he tried to inhale. He could tell that he was bleeding, inside and outside, and was surprised that he could actually sense his life draining away. A rattling noise wheezed past his lips.

His parents always preached reincarnation, that he would return to the world in another form after dying. He'd never put much stock in it, especially if it meant that his less-savory life choices meant he'd be returning as something lower than human. As his body shut down, and the world around him grew dark, he realized he was about to find out if they had been right.

CHAPTER TWENTY-TWO

General Vatutin stood by the cage behind the lab and grinned.

Inside, the captured saber-tooth tiger paced the concrete pad. Its tail whipped back and forth, a twitching outlet for the rage that coursed through the animal. This all-powerful king of its realm had been subjugated and confined for the first time in its life. It bared its teeth and hissed at Vatutin.

Popov stepped up beside the general. "That cat is not happy."

"Its spirit must be broken," Vatutin said. "Then it will learn to submit. It will know that the one at the top can become the one at the bottom in a flash."

"The men say they saw the Americans, but they got away."

"The saber-tooth pride attacked and took all of their focus. But I have sent Sergeant Petrov after them. He is my best tracker, my best sniper. He will find them. He will radio in their position to the team I'm about to send out."

Vatutin put a hand on Popov's shoulder. Popov winced with dread.

"You should have been with my men to watch the tiger's glorious capture," Vatutin said.

"I'm not physically strong enough to march through the woods, General."

"I think perhaps not mentally strong enough, either, no? You shy away from this big cat even when it is in a cage."

"We abandoned the big cat research for a good reason. A saber-tooth is like a bomb. It is dangerous by nature."

"And like a bomb," Vatutin said, "harmless when in the right, strong hands, which it is now, in spite of your deceit."

"What do you mean?"

"Popov, you told me of the mammoth research, but made no mention of this glorious cat. If I was a suspicious man, I would say that you were hiding it from me, keeping this prize to yourself."

"General, I assure you. The tiger was one of several previous experiments. All of them were believed to be failures, abandoned to the elements to die. I think the saber-tooth pride was what got into the lab and scattered the team. No mammoth could have gotten there without tearing out a wall. The team in the compound didn't even know there was anything already roaming the island when they introduced mammoths into the valley."

"I wish that I could believe you," Vatutin said. "With the server wiped clean, it is all the more important that I bring this kitty cat back. With all the science that resurrected it gone, he'll have to become the species' new Adam."

At the other end of the cage, the cat lowered its head and locked its eyes on the two men. It assumed a crouching position to pounce.

"Of course, it will be important to keep it healthy," Vatutin said. "I wonder what it eats?"

In an instant, he stepped behind Popov and slammed him face-first against the bars of the cage. He used one hand to press the back of Popov's head so that his nose protruded between the bars and into the cage. Popov yelped.

"Wait," Vatutin said. "I remember what they eat. My men. The ones killed at the mammoth pit by the tigers you supposedly knew nothing about. So, we know they have a taste for human flesh. Let's see if this one has worked up an appetite."

"No!" Popov said in a slurred wail with his mouth compressed against the bars.

Vatutin raised up a knee and pressed it into the small of Popov's back. Then with his free hand he grabbed Popov's elbow, and shoved his arm between the bars of the cage.

The tiger roared and pounced. In one leap, it sailed across the cage and hit the concrete pad as it clamped its jaws around Popov's exposed arm. With its front paws braced against the bars, it jerked its massive head straight back.

Popov's arm ripped free at the socket. Blood pumped like an oil well gusher from his shoulder, and hit the concrete with a splat. The tiger dropped the arm onto the floor. It raised its right paw, and sent four razor sharp claws down the bars that framed Popov's face. The claws ripped through his skin and pulled his nose and face right off his skull. Popov managed one choked scream. It turned into a gurgle, and his struggle against the bars and Vatutin stopped. Vatutin let his corpse slide to the ground.

The tiger chomped on the face that lay on the cage floor. It tossed the skin up into the air, opened its jaws wider than seemed possible, and caught the face on its tongue. With one swallow, it was gone. The tiger leapt at the severed arm, and pinned it to the floor with one paw. It began to tear the flesh away with its teeth.

A soldier came jogging up to the cage. He looked down with confusion at Popov's mangled body.

"I heard roaring, General," the soldier explained.

"There was an unfortunate accident. Popov got a little too friendly with one of his cats."

The private stood there, glancing between the corpse and Vatutin.

"Well, toss the rest of him in there and let the tiger finish the job," Vatutin said. "And be quick about it. We need to kill the Americans before we can go home."

And once Sgt. Petrov radioed in the Americans' positions, he'd have Sgt. Basilov lead this next patrol. It was time his men saw what "ruthless" really meant.

CHAPTER TWENTY-THREE

Sgt. Petrov loved being a sniper.

He never shared this story of his youth with other soldiers, but as a child, he'd studied to play the harp. In a post-Soviet world, his mother had purchased one similar to the one she had played when young, under her own mother's instruction. Having her son continue in that tradition meant everything to her.

But it turned out to be more than just carrying on tradition. She didn't just teach him to play, she nurtured his inherent talent. And Petrov had as much of it as his mother. She claimed he had more.

He'd relished the harp for its simplicity and precision. Each string was one note, fine-tuned by the strength of his own touch. And unlike large percussion instruments and much of the brass, the harp could stand alone, shine without accompaniment. All it took to excel was to focus on his own actions.

Conscription had forced him into the Russian Army and required the trading of his harp for an assault rifle. Just as he'd resigned himself to enduring his compulsory military sidetrack, he had been introduced to the position of sniper. Here he could rise above the blunt-force ideology of the Russian infantry and embrace again the concepts of precision and finesse. Each target was a single harp string, each uniquely set up for the kill. He likened that process to deciding exactly how his fingers would pluck a harp string.

An infantryman followed orders and bumbled into committing manslaughter. The sniper made a plan and performed an execution.

His skill with a sniper rifle had gotten him noticed. Recruitment into the Spetsnaz, a military wing of the Russian GRU followed. There he found he wasn't only good at his job, he loved it.

When he'd been assigned to deploy with General Vatutin, he'd assumed this mission would be no different from any other. He'd been very wrong. Hunting woolly mammoths and saber-tooth tigers weren't two of the GRU's usual tasks, and he was up for neither. Based on a mammoth's size, his one bullet wasn't going to even slow them down.

But when he'd gotten this current mission from General Vatutin a few hours ago, he'd relaxed. His orders were to track down some good-old-fashioned human targets.

He first figured out where the Americans would be going. They'd want to escape, and a route down the valley through ice and snow to the frozen sea would be suicide. The Americans would climb, likely to the lake first, then to the flat, open area on the mountainside below the snowline. It was the only place other than the airfield where a helicopter or a plane could land.

He mapped out the likely route a group would take to get to the lake. Then he figured out the fastest one an individual could take. Even if they had a head start, they would have rested for the night before continuing on. He could catch up.

And a few hours into his hunt, he was certain he had caught up. He'd nestled into a rocky niche that overlooked where a wildfire had burned away the forest and left a rough rectangle about a hundred meters long on the wider side. The trail the Americans would be following ran through the center of the burn.

His mission was to radio back the Americans' position and await the reinforcement squad for the attack. And of course he'd do that first part. But if the Americans attacked him first, he would have to defend himself. And his story was going to be that the Americans attacked him first.

The burned-over area offered nowhere to hide, nowhere to run to. In Petrov's experience, when under fire, civilians without military training tended to freeze in place. After he dropped the first one, he'd probably be able to finish the rest of the group before anyone took flight.

He shot a laser rangefinder to the trail to get the distance. Then he took an estimate of the light breeze. He dialed corrections into his rifle's scope, and then used it to scan the trail. Nothing there now.

But there soon would be. And then Petrov would begin plucking strings.

#

Grant breathed a sigh of relief as the narrow trail opened up to a wide clearing. Deborah had been walking ahead of him, and sending flexed branches swinging back and slapping him in the face for an hour. A break from that just might keep him from exploding at her.

Williams stopped at the clearing's edge. The rest of the group crowded in behind him. The former field had turned to blackened ash. A few tree stumps and charred logs dotted the space. About halfway across rose a rock pyramid trail marker.

"What's the hold up?" Destro said.

"One clearing was full of sleeping saber-tooths," Williams said. "Another was a poison gas trap. A little caution wouldn't hurt crossing a third."

Destro looked out across the charred field. "No mammoths, obviously. Everything has been burned to ash, so there's nowhere for tigers to hide. The Russians are busy behind us capturing specimens. We have a schedule to meet. Move out."

Williams gave Destro the same look Grant gave his department dean every time the man displayed his ignorance by making a bad decision. Kai stepped past Williams and into the clearing.

"I was here when we put out this fire a few months ago," he said. "The trail's marked. Never seen animal signs here. It's safe."

Kai headed out across the clearing. Destro gave Williams an "Are you going to follow him?" look. Williams shook his head and headed down the trail. The rest of the group followed with Destro last in line.

The hazy sun hit Grant's face and the warmth felt fantastic. Not as fantastic as it would on the beach at Waikiki, but a welcome break from the shade of the forest they'd been trekking through. If Kai was correct and there were never any animal traces in this clearing, there was a chance that due to altitude or some other territorial quirk in the creatures, Grant's group might have hiked outside their range. Maybe all that was left was a short walk up to the plateau, the rescue plane zooming in—

From up ahead, Kai's voice interrupted his fantasy. He was almost out of the clearing. "See, guys. No danger here at all."

A rifle shot cracked from over Grant's right shoulder. Kai's chest exploded in a spray of crimson. His body spun around and then collapsed onto the grass.

Grant, Deborah, Connor, and Destro froze in place. Grant couldn't process the unreal event that just happened before his eyes.

Williams sprinted for the forest. A second shot rang out. Williams cried out and fell into the shadows of the trees.

Grant dropped to the ground. The others had beat him to it. Deborah had found a charred tree stump to use as cover. Destro had scrambled up behind a rock a little bigger than a basketball. Connor was crawling toward where they'd entered the clearing as fast as he could without taking his chest off the ground. Nothing but a few blades of grass shielded Grant from the shooter.

Destro had the stock of his AK-47 pressed into his shoulder and had the barrel pointing uphill at a collection of boulders.

"Why don't you shoot back?" Grant screamed.

"At what?" Destro said. "I can't see anyone."

A third shot came from the boulders. The bullet zipped by so close to Grant's head that he heard it sing and felt the passage of its heat alongside his temple. A flurry of severed hairs fluttered down onto the back of his hand. He dropped down flatter and wished he could burrow into the soil.

Destro fired three rounds at the boulders. Each sent up a flurry of dust and stone chips. But the shots were all over the place, and none hit the sniper.

Grant saw a mound of earth to his left. He crawled toward it. Just as he moved, the sniper fired again. The bullet sent up a plume of dirt where he'd just been lying.

"Stay right there, Manwich," Deborah said. "Keep drawing his fire."

Grant rolled over and ended up behind the pile of dirt. It wouldn't stop a bullet, but if he was out of sight, he hoped the sniper would decide to shoot at the loudmouthed woman by the stump instead. Grant certainly would have.

Destro sent a half-dozen rounds in the direction of the boulders. This time several sailed past the rocks without hitting anything.

"Nice shooting," Grant said. "That sniper's going to think twice about jumping six meters in the air."

Before Destro could respond, the sniper fired again. The bullet buried itself in the dirt mound shielding Grant.

The impact exploded the mound. It wasn't rock, it wasn't even hard-packed earth. The mound was an insect nest, honeycombed with passages, and those passages were filled with millipedes. Dirt and millipedes and a nursery of millipede eggs sprayed Grant in the face.

A swarm of millipedes seemed to be everywhere in an instant. They crawled through his hair, zipped across his face, climbed up his arms. One raced across his lips and he tried to blow it away.

Grant reacted without thinking. He screamed and jumped to his feet. He swiped and swatted at the army of insects that crawled over his skin and under his clothes. He heard the amplified crunch of one crawling into his ear and shrieked again.

He expected the next sound to be the crack of a rifle to end his miserable torture. Instead, his scream was answered by another from the boulders. He finished brushing away most of the millipedes and looked at the boulders above them. Williams slowly rose from behind the rocks. His rifle was slung across his shoulders. He held his machete in one hand. Blood ran down the blade, over the hilt, and dripped from his fingers.

Williams picked his way through the boulders, then downhill to the group. He carried a military vest in his other hand. Hand grenades and ammunition magazines bulged from the pouches. Deborah and Destro stood up. Connor jogged over from the woods.

"That was an exceptionally manly display," Deborah said to Grant. "The shriek wasn't girly at all."

"It was just the right amount of calculated overreaction to distract the sniper so Williams could sneak up on him," Grant said. "You're welcome."

Williams staggered over to Destro. His face was white. He held the vest up for Destro to see.

"Russian sniper," he said. "Tough son of a bitch. If they sent him, more will be right behind him. No time to waste."

"Agreed," Destro said.

Williams put the sniper's vest on. The machete hung up on the vest, so Williams turned the big blade over to Destro. Destro held the handle at the far end to keep from touching the blood on it. He wiped it across the ground a few times to clean it. Williams rolled his eyes, then handed Destro the machete's scabbard. Destro hooked it to his belt and sheathed the blade.

Williams then led the group through the wildfire burn. They came to Kai's body. There was a gaping hole in his chest that revealed a mass of red and black churned organs. At least the bookkeeper didn't know what hit him.

Destro flipped the body over and shoved a hand into Kai's back pocket. He pulled out the rough map the man had made with all his annotations. Destro shoved the paper into his own pocket.

"That's it?" Grant said. "Nothing to say about the dead man at your feet?"

"Sure," Destro said. "I need his map."

Grant wanted to punch Destro, but the AK in the man's hands helped keep Grant's temper in check. Grant took the lead heading up the trail, willing to trade the danger of being first for being as far away as possible from Destro. Connor ran up to join him.

"That was hairy," Connor said. "Those millipedes looked pretty gross."

"Imagine how gross they felt."

"I'd have screamed too, if they were all over me."

Grant was now getting condescending sympathy from a kid who thought his hack writing was literary genius. This trip just got better every minute.

Destro's safari party had now left five corpses behind on their attempt to escape Mammoth Island. Grant wondered if whatever deity ruled this place would accept that as enough sacrifice to ensure that the rest of them survived.

But so far, their sacrifices hadn't seemed to reap any rewards.

#

Vatutin did not tolerate waiting well. The anticipation of Sgt. Petrov's update taxed his minimal patience. He strode over to the radio operator set up at one of the lab benches.

"Hasn't Petrov called in an update yet?"

"No, General. Not since he reported setting up at the wildfire burn."

"Raise Petrov on the radio."

The radio operator called out to the sniper. There was no response. He tried twice more with the same result.

Vatutin picked up some laboratory glassware from a countertop and threw it across the room. It shattered against the wall. All activity in the lab stopped and every soldier looked at the general.

He took a deep breath and togged the bottom of his tunic to smooth the wrinkles.

"When a jeweler's screwdriver fails," he announced, "then it's time to use a sledgehammer. Sergeant Brusilov!"

The stout NCO ran up in front of the general and came to attention.

"Sergeant," Vatutin said, "take a team into the forest. Find and kill those Americans. When we depart, I don't want anyone left alive on this island."

CHAPTER TWENTY-FOUR

Williams led them through the forest for a while and then the group came to the wide, stony banks of a fast-running stream. Destro took out the map Kai had drawn. Blood stained the map's lower edge.

"This is the stream we're looking for," Destro said. "It runs from the lake all the way down to the compound."

"This will be the fastest route to the lake," Williams said.

The stream banks were much wider than Grant would have thought given the narrow waterway. The group trudged uphill with the water on their left.

Half an hour later, they came to the base of a dam that rose about ten meters high between the steepening streambanks. Water from the lake behind it fed the stream from a small spillway to the left. Boulders made up the foundation at the dam's base, but the rest of the construction consisted of pine logs. They were not stacked neatly one upon the other, but more arranged to fit, like rocks in a stone fence, with clearly discernable gaps between many logs. Somehow, no water leaked out.

"Looks more like a sieve than a dam," Destro said.

"But it's working," Deborah said as she gave the structure a visual inspection. "Kai didn't say this lake was artificial."

"It looks like the dam has been here a while," Grant said. "Before this last bunch of scientists arrived."

The group picked their way up the hillside to the right of the dam. Grant had to drop to hands and knees in places to keep from sliding back down. He wheezed as he struggled up the slope. Deborah looked back at him with disdain.

"Damn," she said. "You know, getting some regular exercise wouldn't hurt you."

"You'd be surprised what a low threshold for pain I have."

At the top of the dam, its breadth became apparent. The structure was four meters wide. Mud and smaller branches covered the lakeside surface and the top of the dam.

Deborah nodded to the structure with admiration. "Now this is impressive."

"It's a pile of big sticks," Grant said.

"It looks like a log jam," Connor said.

"But it isn't," Deborah said. "The people building this dam used all local materials. They thought through placement of logs based on size and length to create a strong, woven, dual-walled structure. Then they waterproofed and reinforced the upstream wall with mud. That's a hell of a feat all cut off from the rest of the world. I'd like to meet the engineer who put this wonder together."

A lake spread out behind the dam, filling the valley at least two kilometers across. The tops of dead pines stuck out of the water at random intervals. About halfway across, the mound of a small island rose in the lake. Grass covered its irregular surface and a few pioneering saplings had volunteered to start a grove near its center. At the lake's far side, the valley wall rose up into the capping mist that kept this warmer world separate from the icy wasteland beyond. A waterfall cascaded down the slope into the river.

"The glacier melts at the edge of this warm zone and keeps fresh water flowing," Deborah said. "I'm impressed."

It was clear where all the trees to build the dam had come from. The shore around the lake was a stubble of rotting stumps where the builders had slashed down trees for its construction. Patchy grass grew between the stumps. Here and there, geothermal vents released trickles of steam from the ground. Smaller logs and leftover scraps littered the shoreline or bobbed just offshore in the still lake.

"This water has to be cold as hell," Grant said.

He went down to the lake and stuck in a finger. He expected it to be ice water, but it was surprisingly warm.

"Wow, warm," he said. "Constant sun and geothermal heating likely keep it at a decent temperature."

"Now that I think about it," Deborah said, "why create this lake? It isn't generating power. There's no need for flood control. It seems like a lot of wasted effort."

"Lakefront property," Grant said. "Put in a hotel and a casino, and the tourists will come. Until they start getting eaten by saber-tooth tigers."

Grant remembered that lakefront property was attractive to more than tourists. A stable supply of fresh water attracted animals. And big mammals used up a lot of water wandering around, especially shaggy, bulky mammoths.

Grant searched the ground around the tree stumps. It had been pounded flat over a long period of time. In some places the grass looked newly crushed and big, round prints were stamped in the sand.

"Uh, guys," Grant said. "We should probably—"

The sound of a trumpeting mammoth cut him off.

The eyes of everyone in the group went wide. Grant didn't need to finish the sentence.

CHAPTER TWENTY-FIVE

A tree at the edge of the clearing crashed to the ground and revealed the matriarch of the mammoth herd. She looked just as furious as she had back at the corral. She raised her trunk and let loose a trumpeting so angry that it made Grant shiver.

"Dammit," Destro said. "How did she find us?"

"I'm sure a six-foot long trunk and an olfactory center bigger than your head had nothing to do with it," Grant said.

"Skirt the edge of the lake," Williams said. He aimed his rifle at the matriarch's forehead. "There's only one of them to hold off."

More mammoth trumpeting sounded from along the wood line. Several smaller mammoths appeared to the right and left of the matriarch. The matriarch snorted and locked eyes on Williams.

"Might want to recount that," Grant said.

Mammoths on the far flanks jogged forward to block any escape along the banks of the lake. The matriarch stepped forward and slashed the air with her tusks in a wide figure-eight. Grant remembered how the mammoths had sliced and tortured the scientist from the lab. The matriarch looked like she was warming up to host the same kind of party. Grant had no interest in being one of the guests of honor. But he and the others would never get through the semi-circle the beasts had made around their little lakeshore beachhead.

"The island!" Connor said. "We'll swim for it."

Grant looked across the lake and blanched. It would be a hell of a swim to get there.

"Don't tell me you can't swim," Deborah said. "Weren't you heading to Hawaii before this whole catastrophe unfolded?"

"To sit by the water, not to join the sharks that swim in it. I suppose you're a great swimmer?"

"I do triathlons."

"Of course you do."

Destro grabbed Grant's shoulder. "Can mammoths swim?"

"We're about to find out."

The matriarch lowered her head to charge the group. The rest of the herd held back, as if they knew not to deprive the leader of the first pass at the prey.

Williams let loose a barrage of rounds. They all hit her head dead center. The mammoth shook her head, but it seemed more in frustration than because the bullets had any effect.

Everyone but Williams broke for the water. Deborah dove in and cut through the water like a hot knife through butter. She surfaced and began a front crawl that would make Olympic swimmers jealous. Grant found a new reason to hate the woman.

He ran into the lake, but by his third step, the drag from the deepening water sent him into an unbearable slow motion. Another round of onshore gunfire added to his fear. He raised both hands to execute a dive like Deborah had.

Instead, he belly-flopped. Then he began an uncoordinated set of arm and leg motions that churned water far better than it propelled him forward. But now the water was over his head, and there was certainly no turning back. His entire body began to feel tired.

Just ahead, a log floated in the lake. The barrel-sized section of tree trunk looked like it might keep him above water. He switched to an embarrassing dog-paddle stroke so he wouldn't lose sight of the log. The struggle to keep his head above the waves reaped the reward of a mouthful of lake water. He spat it out and gagged. For a lake refilled by fresh ice melt, the water sure tasted like hell.

The paddling got harder. His muscles burned from the unaccustomed exercise and threatened to let him sink to the bottom for harassing them like this. The waterlogged shoes on his feet felt like lead weights. He closed on the floating log. More gunfire and the roars of mammoths filled the air.

Grant reached out and slapped one hand against the log. It slid back down across bark slickened by algae. His head dipped underwater.

He kicked his feet and resurfaced. With an exhale like a breaching dolphin, he grabbed for the log with both hands. His fingers found the nubs of broken branches and he gripped the log with all the strength he had left. He kicked and pulled himself up until his shoulders came full out of the water. The log submerged under his weight, but not completely. The centimeters that remained above water would be just enough to keep him from drowning.

Grant looked around him. Deborah was already almost to the island. Connor and Destro had found similar makeshift life rafts and were paddling to the safe haven. Weighted down with a rifle and machete, Destro was struggling on his log, but he was making progress. He was apparently willing to let Williams sacrifice himself for his own survival. The bastard.

Back on shore, mammoths splashed at the edge of the lake. The herd members reared up on their back legs and then came down into the lake on their front. They screamed and trumpeted, furious that their prey was getting away.

In the center, the matriarch had squared off one-on-one with Williams. All the gunfire hadn't fazed the creature. Williams dropped his rifle and plucked a grenade from his liberated sniper's vest. He pulled the pin.

The matriarch charged. Williams threw the grenade. Without missing a beat, the mammoth swept back its trunk, and then batted away the flying explosive. It sailed into the lake with a splash. The grenade detonated underwater, and sent a plume of frothy spray up into the air.

Williams' jaw dropped at the mammoth's deflection of the grenade. He reached down for his rifle.

But he was too late. The mammoth was on him. The beast reared back and then slashed him across both legs with its tusk. Blood gushed and bones snapped. Williams collapsed with a scream.

Fury burned bright in the mammoth's eyes. It wrapped its trunk around Williams' waist and threw him up in the air. The rifle flew out of Williams' hand and into the lake. As Williams spun, the sniper's vest tore loose and sailed off to the left. Williams hit a terrifying apogee and for the smallest fraction of a second, hung in the air like a superhero. Then he fell straight down. His body landed on one of the rotting stumps and the sharpened tip punched through his body. He didn't move.

Grant turned his focus back to getting to the island. He willed his weakening legs to keep kicking as he followed the rest of the group to the island's shore. By the time he arrived, the others had dragged themselves out of the lake. He paddled until his log ran aground in a few centimeters of water. His knees hit the bottom and he crawled away from the log and then up the muddy bank. Once he was clear of the water, he rolled onto his back in a panting, exhausted heap.

Deborah stepped over and stared down at him. "You made it. Good thing fat floats."

Grant opened his mouth for a smart-ass reply, but he didn't have the strength. Instead, he closed his eyes and gave thanks that he wasn't on the lake shore being pounded into ground meat by mammoths.

CHAPTER TWENTY-SIX

On the shore of the lake, the mammoths splashed knee-deep in the water and slapped their trunks against the surface. The matriarch bellowed out trumpeting so loud that the water rippled around her feet.

"Question answered," Connor said. "Looks like mammoths can't swim."

"From the look of them," Grant said, "if they could, they'd be stomping us into the ground with glee."

Destro dropped the magazine from his rifle, cleared it, and blew some water out of the chamber. He reloaded the weapon, then checked the machete on his belt. Grant wished all that weight had sucked him under on the swim over.

Connor began to climb the slight rise to the island's low peak.

As Destro looked over at Williams' corpse on the far shore, his face painted a portrait of abject misery.

"So," Grant said, "if you were going to sum up our situation in one word, how does 'screwed' work for you?"

"Shut the hell up," Destro said. "I need to think."

"Why didn't you give that a shot before you took us on this vacation to Hell?"

Destro pointed his rifle in Grant's direction. "It would probably be easier with one less person in this group."

"Oh, but not me. I'm your mammoth expert."

"At least mammoth-sized," Deborah said.

Grant turned to Deborah. "Can we please focus our abuse on the guy wearing the black hat in this Western?"

Destro pulled the handheld radio from the pocket of his cargo pants and turned it on. It came to life with a short burst of static. Destro keyed the mic and a needle on the radio bounced.

"Pays to buy military-grade," he said. "This still works, which means I can still redirect the plane to the plateau. Don't make yourself such a hinderance that I don't save you a seat home."

"One small item in our way between now and then," Grant said. "This lake. Oh, and maybe the mammoths on the shore."

The mammoths had moved north, to a point closer to the island. The deep water was still an obstacle, or at least Grant hoped so.

He'd recovered a bit from the swim over, and stood up to let some of the water drain out of his clothes. He was about to take off his shirt to wring it out, then realized that would set Ms. Fitness Freak on another rant about his physique. He kept his shirt on and tried to squeeze some water out of the front of it.

The ground beneath him seemed oddly irregular. He scraped away some of the mossy surface with his shoe and uncovered pine bark. Further scraping revealed it was a tree trunk mostly buried in silty earth. Some of the trees felled while making the dam had washed up here. That made sense. The only island in the lake would snag a lot of what drifted from the shore over the years.

Connor came scrambling down from the island's peak. "There's a kind of cave or tunnel or something up there."

"The builders made a cave?" Grant said.

"It looks like it. It's lined with wood like the dam is."

"A little shelter wouldn't hurt my feelings," Deborah said.

"And we could use a rest," Grant said. "Perpetual daylight is fooling us, but we've been awake a long time, with little sleep."

"And maybe 'out-of-sight' means 'out-of-mind' for the mammoths," Connor said, "and they will leave."

Destro checked his watch. "But we still have hours to go before the plane is back in radio range. That cave is as good a place as any to hole up until the mammoths get bored of waiting. No point in having the Russians see us sitting out here as sniper targets, either."

They followed Connor uphill. Near the top, they came to an opening about two meters around. A meter in, the cave sloped down and disappeared into darkness. Humid, earthy air drifted out of the mouth.

"Everyone in," Destro said.

Grant stepped inside with the others. The walls looked like mostly tree trunks and heavy branches. Moss grew from every crevice. He clicked the flashlight Kai had handed out earlier. The beam didn't travel all the way to the back of the cave. Deborah turned her flashlight on and illuminated the wall in front of her. She ran her hands over the logs.

"This isn't random," she said. "It's like the dam, specifically constructed and reinforced."

"If seven dwarfs come marching out," Grant said, "first dibs on the diamonds and jewels."

"There had to be a reason the scientists invested the effort," Destro said.

"Who wouldn't want a nice getaway spot like this by a lake," Grant said. "With a view of the mammoths waiting to kill you."

"Maybe they hid something here," Connor said. "Stored it for safekeeping from the creatures that roamed the island."

"This island isn't on Kai's map," Destro said. "He would have mentioned it if it was important."

"Maybe he didn't know about it," Grant said. "No one mentioned *Smilodons* and they're here."

"All of this was built by the earlier group," Destro said. "If they stored secrets of what they did on this island, my trip here might not have been a total waste."

Grant took a seat on the ground. "We wouldn't want that. Take a look, tell us what you find. I'll stay here and guard the fresh air and daylight."

Destro pointed the rifle at Grant. "You're going to tell me if what we find is important. I think we should stick together. I insist."

"I wonder how persuasive you are without that rifle to back you up?" Grant said.

Destro shouldered the rifle, reached down and yanked Grant up by his shirt collar. Destro pulled the machete from his belt and lay it across Grant's chest.

"Well?" he said.

"You know," Grant said, "you're still surprisingly persuasive."

"Why don't you go first?"

"Rhetorical question?"

"Absolutely." Destro turned to the others. "The rest of you stay here."

"I'll go with you," Connor said. "You might need help carrying out anything you find."

Grant led Destro and Connor into the cave's deeper recesses. The passage took a steeper downward slope and Grant had to steady himself against the wall for better balance.

"This is like in your book *Cavern of the Damned*," Connor said.

"God, I hope not."

Then the shaft took a sharp bend and went straight down. Grant shined his light down the opening. The shaft stopped about ten meters down. Destro stuck his head over Grant's shoulder.

"What are you waiting for?" he said.

"An elevator to be installed."

"Go!" Destro said

"Sure, I'll just jump for it."

"Climb down, you idiot."

Grant shined his light on the shaft walls. The nubs and bits of branches stuck from the shaft like pins from a pincushion. There were plenty to use for hand and footholds all the way down. His real worry was having to use them all the way back up.

One hand and then one foot at a time, Grant eased his way down the shaft with Connor lighting the way with his flashlight. Destro was right behind him, almost crushing Grant's hands with every step down.

"Dammit," Destro said. "Could you move any slower?"

"Yes, of course, if that would make you happier."

"Get moving before I stomp your fingers and send you to the bottom in a hurry."

The rising air was much more pronounced here, and the smell, that had at first seemed just musty, now dialed in closer to the scent of a dock on a freshwater lake, a combination of algae, fish, and decay.

"Whatever stinking thing these guys hid down here," Grant said to himself, "I am not hauling it back up."

He finally got near the bottom of the shaft, and jumped down the last meter. Grant landed with the sound of snapping branches, and he sank a few centimeters into the surface.

"Move it!" Destro said.

Grant stepped aside as Destro dropped to the ground beside him. Grant turned on his flashlight.

They stood on a platform of branches and sticks, held together with a brownish silt. The platform stretched out about two hundred square meters. The cavern-like space they stood in was about two meters high and extended twice as far as the platform. Water filled the space past the platform's edge.

"What the hell did those crazy Russians build here?" Destro said.

"Shine a light up here so I can see to climb down," Connor said from the shaft.

Grant stuck his head up the shaft. "Hold up. It might not be worth the trip."

Destro stepped down to the water's edge. His feet sank into the oozing platform with every step.

Grant played his flashlight's beam along the wall, revealing more logs and branches. The whole thing looked very familiar, on a smaller scale. He couldn't place it.

"Unless these Russians had a fetish about building with Lincoln Logs and Tinker Toys," Grant said, "they didn't build this. And I haven't seen any dirt or stone anywhere. I don't think this is an island."

"It's in the middle of a damn lake. What the hell else would you call it?"

Grant knelt down and scooped up some of the silt between the branches. He sniffed it and then instantly pulled his face away. It stank like an uncleaned fish tank, or more precisely, like an exhibit he'd seen at his local zoo on fresh water mammals.

In a flash, he remembered why this looked so familiar.

"We need to get the hell out of here," Grant said.

"Now?"

"Five minutes ago would have been better, but I'll settle for now. Something lives in here. Something big."

"Like what?"

The water churned and sent waves crashing against the platform. Something struck the platform hard enough to make it shake. Grant and Destro grabbed the walls for support. A dark mass rose out the water.

Grant knew he was going to hate himself for doing it, but he pointed his flashlight's beam across the water.

Two brown eyes lit up in the light. A furry head twice as big as a human's surfaced. It had fat cheeks and oversized front teeth that protruded from its top and bottom lips. The corners of its lips curled up in a sneer. A wide, flat tail broke the surface behind it and slapped the water hard enough to send a wave against the room's far wall. The wave reflected back and slammed into the platform.

Grant was face to face with the world's biggest beaver, and it looked pissed.

CHAPTER TWENTY-SEVEN

Grant knew that giant beavers had once roamed North America. Over two meters long and weighing in at over 140 kilos, they would put current beavers to shame. In other circumstances, this amazing underground discovery would have made him ecstatic.

In these circumstances, it made him terrified.

"What the hell?" Destro said.

"Another experiment gone bad," Grant said. He started to climb back up the shaft.

Destro leveled his rifle at the beaver. The creature hissed and began a charge up the platform. Destro pulled the trigger. The rifle's report echoed in the confined space and sent a flurry of twigs and dead leaves cascading from the ceiling.

The round hit the beaver in the head right above the eyes. Blood splashed all over its fur. The beaver staggered, recovered slightly, and took another step forward. Destro fired another round into its skull. The second shot blew half its cranium away and the beaver dropped to the ground. More leaves and twigs rained down from overhead.

"Grant!" Connor shouted from the top of the shaft. "What's happening?"

"We're fine," Destro shouted back. He turned to Grant. "See, Chicken Little, modern firepower beats…whatever that is."

Grant stepped over to the dead beaver. He focused his flashlight on its eyes. No reaction. He played it on the back of its head where a gaping hole exposed a pile of mushy gray matter. While every horror movie he'd ever seen had taught him that no monster is ever really dead, he was sure this one was.

The beaver was over two meters long. Grant estimated that the bulky thing had to weigh well over 100 kilos. In his mind he heard Deborah say "That thing's almost as big as you." He hated hearing Deborah's voice saying anything, especially in his head.

"This is a *Castoroides ohioensis*," Grant said. "A species of extinct giant beaver. Popov's men didn't build this dam, a beaver did. And we aren't on an island. This is a classic beaver lodge, scaled up by a factor of a hundred or so. Beavers swim in from underwater and live here. We climbed down an air shaft."

"Ugh. That means this gritty stuff on my boots is…"

"Beaver poo. Enjoy."

"How many 'failed' experiments did Popov set free in this valley?" Destro said.

"Much as I'm a fan of scientific breakthroughs," Grant said, "I'm okay with this being the last one we find."

Destro gave the beaver a closer look. "That thing is huge."

It was larger than the fossils Grant had read about. But even with that, he couldn't imagine it manhandling the larger tree trunks in the dam into place. And while the beaver was big, this was way too large a lodge for one animal. Nature abhorred waste, and this busy beaver hadn't built himself a mansion to impress the neighbors.

"I have a bad feeling," Grant said as he stepped away from the shore.

The water churned again, this time far stronger than the last time, and across a wider area. Destro retreated to the air shaft.

"There's more than one beaver," Grant said.

Four heads popped up out of the water. The beavers looked at their dead compatriot, then all eyes turned to Grant and Destro.

Grant feared that multiple shots from Destro's rifle would bring so much of the roof down they might be crushed. He turned to warn him.

He was just in time to see Destro disappear as he scurried up the air shaft. Bits of branches rained down onto the ground.

"Son of a …" Grant ran for the shaft.

Behind him, the water exploded in a flurry of splashes. He wasn't going to turn around and check it out. He was willing to assume four giant beavers were out to kill him.

Platform branches cracked and rustled as the creatures closed in on him. Grant jammed his flashlight in his shirt pocket with the lens facing up and dashed to the bottom of the shaft. As his panting chest heaved, his flashlight beam alternated between a poor view of the shaft and half blinding him. He searched for a hand hold. Nothing. He'd jumped down the last meters on the way in. His gut sank as he realized there might not be one, or if there had been, Destro might have snapped it off in his panicked climb out.

He was going to have to make one.

He found a mud-packed gap between two branches and jammed his hand inside. The contents felt gooey and he remembered what made up a good bit of this beaver den. He shuddered, reached up, and punched his hand into another crevice. This one wasn't as wide, and skin scraped off his knuckles. He yelped and imagined a hundred fatal micro-organisms entering his bloodstream.

He pulled himself up as his feet windmilled for purchase at the base of the shaft. The toe of his right shoe caught something and he dug in. He looked up. Another chunk of debris knocked loose by Destro's boot smacked him in the face. He spat something nasty out of his mouth. At this rate an infection might kill him before the beavers did.

He pulled himself up another meter just as a beaver slammed into the wall at the base of the shaft. Branches snapped and the vibration loosened a torrent of debris from above him. Grant closed his eyes and hoped Destro wasn't going to be part of it. He found a handhold and pulled himself up through the earthy hailstorm.

Below, a chorus of hissing echoed in the chamber. Grant climbed up another step as a beaver jammed its head into the shaft after him. A whoosh of thick, fishy air blew up past Grant. Its nose shoved against Grant's shoe. Only the narrowness of the shaft kept the beaver from opening its mouth and chomping down on Grant's foot.

He kept climbing. The sound of the beavers running around the platform below grew fainter. His whole body ached in objection to this activity. He paused and braced himself against the shaft with his back. He took a deep breath. A stick hit him on the head, bounced between his legs, and tumbled down into the den. A beaver hissed.

"Grant?" Connor said. His voice was closer than Grant had dreamed possible.

"I'm okay. Be right there."

He continued scaling the shaft. A few exhausting minutes later he got to where it curved closer to level. Connor grabbed his shoulders and pulled him the rest of the way out.

As he balanced on the edge of the shaft, the floor beneath him gave way. Connor gripped Grant's wrist and pulled him forward as the area around the air shaft collapsed, followed by a section of the roof overhead. When the dust settled, branches and sticks blocked the air shaft.

Destro stood a few meters closer to the opening, wiping dirt off his shirt.

"That was too close," Grant said to Connor. "Thanks."

He looked to Destro, who had transitioned to wiping dirt from his pants.

"Big thanks to you, too," he deadpanned. "I never could have made it out without you."

"Hell, if I'd waited for you to go first, I'd be beaver food down there right now."

While that was probably true, Grant certainly wasn't going to admit it. Connor helped Grant to his feet.

"What was down there?" Connor said.

"Giant prehistoric beavers," Grant said.

"Hmm," Connor said. "This is one of the times I can't tell if you're serious."

"This is one of the times I wish I wasn't."

The two of them followed Destro to the mouth of the air shaft. Deborah sat there looking at the mammoths milling about at the lake's edge, apparently unaware of their brush with death. Deborah turned and looked at Grant and Destro.

"You're a mess," she said. "What happened down there?"

"*Castoroides ohioensis*," Grant said. "Another surprise from Popov. Giant beavers, and we're sitting on top of their lodge."

"Don't worry," Destro said. "They can't get up that shaft."

Four beaver heads broke the surface of the lake near the base of the lodge.

"They don't have to," Grant said.

The beavers swam to the lodge and clawed their way out of the lake. They hissed and began to climb in the group's direction.

CHAPTER TWENTY-EIGHT

"Those things are huge!" Connor said.

"Shoot the damn things!" Deborah said to Destro.

"Not enough ammo," Destro said.

The beavers came charging up the side of the lodge in a raccoon-like gallop. With no cover available outside, the four humans retreated into the cave. Connor caught a foot on an exposed branch and hit the ground hard. Grant knelt to help him up.

"You okay?"

"I just twisted the hell out of my ankle."

"We'll barricade the entrance," Deborah said.

"Anything the four of us together could manhandle into place," Grant said, "one of those beavers could toss aside."

Grant helped Connor hobble deeper into the cave. They stopped beside Deborah and Destro at the pile of debris blocking the air shaft.

At the cave entrance, a beaver appeared. It poked its head in and hissed. The creature's white incisors looked well-sharpened from felling trees. It took one step in. The opening was wider than the air shaft had been. There was no saving the group this time.

Destro leveled his rifle and took a quick shot at the beaver. The deafening boom of the report hurt Grant's ears. A shower of debris rained down from the concussion. The round hit the beaver near the shoulder. It flinched, but did not retreat. It growled and filled the air with the disgusting stench of rotting wood.

Grant made several frantic passes around the cave with his flashlight's beam, looking for any kind of escape route. The air shaft was blocked, and that had been the only way out. None of them were going to leave this cave alive.

From across the lake came a high-pitched cry, followed by the trumpeting of mammoths. Just outside the cave, the other three beavers wailed a chorused alarm. The beaver in the tunnel backed out, turned around, and disappeared.

The four humans exhaled a collective sigh of relief. They made their way back to the mouth of the cave, with Connor using the wall as a crutch to keep weight off his injured ankle.

On the far bank of the lake, farther away from where the mammoths had attacked them, a half-sized beaver cowered on the ground. It wailed a terrified cry. Encircling it stood several of the mammoths from the attacking herd, though the matriarch was missing. The mammoths stomped back and forth, blocking the young beaver's escape every time it moved to flee. Whichever way the beaver faced, the mammoth to its rear would slap the beaver's back with its trunk. The beaver would turn around, only to be tagged again from behind by another.

Grant had seen the herd torture the captured scientists. Even without the matriarch's leadership, these six looked ready to do the same to the young beaver.

The four beavers that had been defending the lodge seemed to agree. All were churning through the water, a third of the way across the lake to rescue the youngster.

"What do you know," Grant said. "The mammoths saved us."

"For now," Destro said. "But those things will be back."

"This is our chance to escape," Connor said.

"And get killed by the Russians," Grant said. "They must have caught up with us by now."

Grant looked out across the lake and had a horrible idea.

"We could end all of this," he said, "if we breached the dam. All this water would flood the valley, destroy the compound, crush the Russian planes."

"It would do worse than that," Deborah said. "If you flood that geothermal generator and short out all the safeties, the thing will overload and 'boom'."

"And that would be how big a boom?"

"Earthquake level boom."

"That's a big boom."

"How do you plan on breaching the dam?" Destro said.

"*I*, myself, don't plan on breaching anything. But there were grenades in the sniper's vest that Williams had. Someone could grab that vest, set the grenades in the base of the dam, and make the world's biggest water slide all the way to the valley floor."

Along the lake, the beavers made it to the shoreline. They bobbed in the water, screaming at the mammoths. One of the mammoths stepped forward and stomped on the small beaver's tail to hold it in place. The creature yelped and flailed its paws against the mud. The rest of the mammoths formed a line along the water between the beavers and their young.

"Those things aren't content with just torturing that little beaver," Deborah said. "They want to make sure the others see them do it."

"The basic good nature you see in elephants," Grant said, "was never bred into this species. They are fundamentally malevolent. Another reason nothing in this valley can ever be let loose in the world."

"Then you'd better get swimming," Destro said.

"I'm really more the idea man, preferring to leave the execution to others."

Destro raised his rifle. "I'm the man with the gun, the one who can do executions. I'm not swimming over there. And Connor's ankle means he isn't doing it."

"You're assuming The Incredible Bulk can even make it over there," Deborah said. "Swimming here almost killed him."

"Thank you for testifying to my lack of fitness," Grant said.

"Your emasculation is my pleasure." Deborah turned to Destro. "I'll do it instead."

"No way. If he fails, I'll need your expertise to make a Plan B. That makes Grant the expendable one to try this longshot plan."

At the lake side, one of the beavers had galloped ashore to try an end run around the mammoths' defensive line. The mammoths stomped around the shore in response. The baby beaver wailed as the mammoth pinning it pressed down harder.

"Get going," Destro said as he pointed the rifle at Grant, "while all the wildlife is distracted."

It was now or never to give his plan a try. "Never" didn't sound that bad as he envisioned being attacked by a beaver on the way over, or eviscerated by a mammoth tusk when he got there. But if he didn't try, whatever beavers survived the mammoth attack would be back to finish them all off.

"I'm expecting all of you to eulogize me as a hero at my funeral," he said.

"Grant," Deborah said, "blow out rocks in the foundation. That will be the easiest way to take it down."

He was shocked at her constructive comment, not to mention using his given name for the first time during this little vacation. "Thanks."

He looked over at the shoreline where beavers feinted at the mammoth defenses and the mammoths countered like some Pleistocene-era dance. They were a long way away from the spot near the dam where Williams had died and the vest lay on the shore. He hoped it was far enough.

Against every ounce of common sense he had, Grant stood, and then skidded downhill to the lake.

CHAPTER TWENTY-NINE

As he approached the water, the cries of the confrontation between the beavers and the mammoths came across the lake loud and clear. That oddly gave him comfort. With those two groups locked in combat, he was much more likely to get to the dam unseen.

At the water's edge, he selected a driftwood log to use as his personal flotation device. He selected one a little narrower than the one he'd floated over on, and one that was a lot less mossy. He'd become a connoisseur of log floats. He rolled the log into the water and waded in after it. Once the water was chest-high, he hopped up across the log and held on tight. It didn't roll over. He began to kick.

Halfway across, an awful thought occurred to him. What if the beavers and mammoths weren't all that the first team had left here? What if they'd stocked this lake with some prehistoric fish? His mind raced through a list of freshwater fossils he'd uncovered over the years. *Mioplosus*, *Phareodus*, *Amia*. His imagination of course went to those predators, and then to visions of being devoured in a feeding frenzy. He rationalized that the compound had no facilities for raising fish. There was no way the scientists would have branched out to fish from mammals.

That didn't stop him from kicking a little harder.

This low in the water, he lost sight of the battle between the giant beasts to the north. But he could still hear it. He wondered how the two sides were faring and what kind of attack the beavers could mount against bulletproof mammoths. If there had been a safe place from which to observe, he'd have loved to have watched. A dozen suppositions about extinct megafauna could have been validated or disproven in minutes.

At the shoreline, the water shallowed enough for him to stand up. He cast away the log and slogged ashore. He'd arrived where they'd escaped the mammoth attack earlier. The herd had trampled the ground and vegetation flat. Off near the trees, the dark shape that was Williams' mangled corpse hung impaled on the tree stump. Grant looked away and began to search for the sniper's vest. He soon found it sticking out of the mud.

He ran over to it. The mammoths had stomped it into the ground. He feared that the behemoths had crushed anything in the vest into useless scrap.

He dug away at the mud with his hands until he could extract the vest. He dropped it on the ground and swept the worst of the mud away. It was a veritable mobile arsenal. The front pockets contained a trio of cylindrical hand grenades. The rear pockets held several magazines of ammunition for a rifle Grant really wished he had. Then he realized the gun wouldn't be any good against a mammoth anyway. However, the idea of shooting Destro, now *that* had its merits.

In another pocket was a pocket knife and a coil of thin wire. He realized that that was for a trip wire to set a grenade as a booby trap. That was a nice find because Grant had been wondering how he was going to set off the grenade in the dam without having to be beside it when he did. Given his horrific experiences in Little League, he knew a precision throw was out of the question. This wire looked long enough that he could be well away from the explosion.

He started to put on the vest, but it reeked pretty badly of lake mud and mammoth feet so he stopped and just held it to his side instead. He jogged over to the end of the dam, and began a hesitant descent down to its base. Over two meters from the bottom, he lost his footing and slid the rest of the way on his butt. He came to a stop in a cloud of dust with a new set of scrapes all along his legs.

"The lesson I'm drawing from this," he said, "is that once I get home, I'm never leaving my house again."

He picked his way along the base of the dam. From a technical perspective, it was a shame to destroy it. A team of scientists could spend months studying the beaver's construction techniques. He stopped near the center where two foundation rocks had a smaller one wedged between them. That looked like the place to set the grenades off. He climbed up the rocks and over the tree trunk laid along them. There was enough space that he could work his way between two logs and drop down to the ground into the space between the inner and outer dam walls.

From the inside, the dam revealed what an engineering marvel it really was. The tree trunks and branches that made up the two walls created a ten-foot-wide open latticework between them that ran all the way to the top of the structure. The logs in the upstream wall were sealed with mud and gravel. The downstream side was a weave of interlocking tree trunks, often with good-sized gaps between them. Water wept from several of the weaker spots in the upstream wall. He was definitely publishing an article on beaver dams if he survived this experience.

He pulled the three grenades from their pouches in the vest. The bodies were caked in mud. He'd learned everything he knew about working with explosives from watching action movies, but he was pretty sure that mud wasn't going to keep these things from exploding. At the top of each cylinder was a ring with a pin on it. A safety handle ran down one side. According to Hollywood, he pulled the pin, the handle popped off, and a few seconds later it went boom. So simple that a child could do it.

I wish Destro was here so I could volunteer him for this, Grant thought.

He crawled over to the weak spot in the foundation. The gaps in the logs left more than enough light in to see what he was doing. He dug away little holes in three spots between the rocks and slipped a grenade into each, leaving the pin and handle exposed. He packed dirt and stones around the body of the grenades. That would keep them in place.

Next, he took the trip wire out of his pocket and tied one end to a grenade pin. Then he ran the wire through the other two pins, tying it off at each one. Now when he yanked the wire, he'd pull out all three pins. Even if one pin didn't pull, the explosion of one grenade ought to set off the others, at least according to everything he remembered from the *Die Hard* movie franchise.

Grant climbed up and out of the dam, carefully trailing the wire behind him. He uncoiled it as he walked along the structure's base. Three meters from the end of the dam, he stopped.

He was out of wire.

This was going to be a problem. Grant might have been stupid enough to blow up a dam with hand grenades, but he wasn't stupid enough to stand in front of it when he did it.

He looked up to the top of the dam. Though there wasn't enough trip wire to get to the side, there was enough to get to the top. He could stand directly above where he'd set the grenades. Then after he pulled the pins, he could run along the top to the safety of the shoreline.

That plan disintegrated under the pounding of a reality check. Climbing. Running. Not dying. Poor execution of the first two meant no execution of the third.

He noticed that the forest had grown silent. The kaiju monster battle along the lake had been resolved one way or another. That left the survivors free to roam around and find Grant. The last thing he wanted here was company.

He checked the distance to the edge of the dam again. Surely, the dam wouldn't collapse all at once. After he pulled the pins, he'd probably have a few seconds to scurry out of the way before the wall of water swept downstream.

Okay, he wasn't any better at scurrying than he was at climbing or running. But he was out of options and time.

With the trip wire wrapped tight in one hand, he inched as far away from the blast zone as he could. He took a deep breath, pulled the wire, and bolted for the slope at the dam's edge.

He counted in his head. *One-one thousand, two-one thousand, three-one thousand.* He made it to the side of the streambed. He heaved himself up the slope. The grenades would go off at any moment. He was going to live through this. He was going to be the hero.

He heard a pop behind him. Not a bang. Not a boom. Then two more pops in close succession. Hell bent as he was on climbing as far away from the dam as possible, he had to glance over his shoulder to the dam's base.

White smoke billowed out from where he'd set the hand grenades.

Something had gone very wrong. He stopped and pulled in the trip wire like he was reeling in a fish. The end arrived with three grenade pins attached to it. They'd all been set off. Were they three duds? Maybe the mud or the mammoth stomping *had* damaged them. What did he know about hand grenades anyway? He cursed under his breath.

The smoke drifted down the streambed and hung like a fog in the depression. The spewing stopped, and Grant decided to see what went wrong. He walked back to the middle of the dam, and climbed in to the place where he'd set the grenades.

All three were still tucked in their holes with the handles on the ground a meter or so away. Smoke had painted the inside of the dam there with a white stripe. Grant had a bad feeling about the grenades.

He knelt beside them and pulled one of them out of the ground. Heat had baked the mud on the outside dry. Grant dusted off the little canister. A white line circled the body. The top had a built-in vent hole, now white as a snow drift.

The grenade Williams had hurled at the mammoths had been high explosive, but the three he'd left in the vest were smoke grenades. Grant hadn't tried to blow up the dam. He'd tried to suffocate it.

"Oh, hell."

As usual, he wasn't going to end up the hero after all. The vest was out of any other useful items. This dam wasn't going anywhere.

Nearly immobilized with dejection, he climbed out of the dam. He knelt to look at the foundation in the vain hope he'd at least done some damage. He hadn't.

A huffing noise sounded behind him. His heart jumped into his throat, and he spun around.

The smoke still covered the valley in a hazy fog. The breeze kicked up and the closest smoke dissipated.

Ten meters away, the matriarch stood in the center of the stream bed, staring straight at Grant. The rest of the smoke evaporated to reveal the remainder of the herd standing a few meters behind her. One scaled the banks on each side and stood guard by the dam's edges.

Grant had no escape.

CHAPTER THIRTY

If there was one bright side to years of multiple near-death experiences, it was that they had honed Grant's fight-or-flight reaction. At least the flight part.

Grant whipped around and climbed back into the dam. As he wedged himself through the gap between two tree trunks, his sweating palms lost their grip. He slipped off the trunk and fell inside the dam. He hit the muddy ground flat on his back.

Advancing mammoth feet pounded the ground outside the dam. A mammoth stopped at the dam and cast into shadow the space where Grant lay. He willed his body to move but he could only rise up on his elbows.

A mammoth trunk poked through the opening between the logs. The tips at the end of the trunk spread wide and the mammoth sucked in air like a vacuum cleaner. The tips closed back up and the trunk dove straight for Grant.

He crab-crawled backwards until his shoulders hit a log and stopped him. The trunk wrapped around his ankle and constricted. It felt like a steel noose. The mammoth pulled Grant's leg off the ground and then up against the logs.

There was no way Grant's body was going to fit through the narrow slit. He feared that the mammoth was going to try to make it happen anyway, and would settle for one body part at a time. He swept the ground on both sides with his hands. He found a short, sharp branch that had broken off one of the tree trunks. He grabbed it and executed the closest thing to a sit-up he'd done in decades.

He grabbed the mammoth's trunk with his left hand. It felt warm and leathery and one-hundred percent muscle. Then with his right hand, he stabbed the trunk with the branch. Over and over, he drove the stick against the mammoth with rapid, overhead swings. The stick didn't penetrate its skin. It was like poking a leather couch with a coffee stirrer.

The mammoth jerked him up higher. His shoulders lifted off the ground. Blood rushed to his head. His heart beat faster.

Grant was going to be killed by an indestructible, deranged Dumbo.

An idea flashed to life. On an elephant, the tips of the truck were ultra-sensitive, the reason it could pick up a single straw of hay with them. He aimed the stick between the two tips at the ends of the mammoth's trunk and drove it down hard.

The mammoth bellowed on the other side of the wall. The logs shook and a blast of hot, swampy air rushed through the gaps in the dam. The trunk relaxed and whipped back through the slit between the logs.

Grant dropped straight down, landing on all the fresh bruises he'd just earned. He groaned. The story of his life. Every victory had to have a bit of defeat attached.

Above him, logs ground against each other and sent a cascade of bark chips down all over him. He looked up to see the mammoth's head pressed against the dam, a single brown eye staring down at him. The mammoth let loose another furious cry.

"Good luck, Jumbo," Grant said. He brandished his little stick like a dagger in a vain attempt to feel powerful. "You can't fit in here."

The trunk darted in through a gap a meter higher up than the first. It wrapped around one of the smaller branches that provided support between the two walls. With a yank, it broke the branch free. The structure moaned and a waterfall of dirt and slivers fell on Grant's chest. The branch shattered as the mammoth wrenched it out of the dam.

This pissed off pachyderm was going to come in and get him. Grant had finally discovered a creature that hated him more than his ex-wife. He looked all around the dam structure for an escape route. The whole construction reminded him of a half-played game of Jenga. Slick moss and algae covered most of the surfaces. There was only one way to escape from the mammoth, and that way was up.

His previously dismissed option of climbing was now the only one he had. Grant pulled himself to his feet, wedged himself into the most open space he could find, and started a mad scramble for foot and hand holds.

He remembered reading once that professional rock climbers always had three points of contact as they reached for a fourth. Those people were never being hunted by a mammoth. Grant grasped and kicked for anything that might hold his weight as he pulled himself higher a few dozen centimeters or less each time.

The mammoth roared and its trunk darted back into the dam wall to the right of Grant's waist. It gripped several support branches at once and pulled. The wood splintered, and the mammoth let the pieces drop. The dam creaked, and the sound echoed all along the structure's interior.

Grant climbed faster. He scraped his fingers and gouged his legs as he struggled to find the next point to grip in the dam. Another few meters up, he came to a wider gap between two logs that gave him a view of the downstream valley. The matriarch stood up against the dam, ripping away logs and branches to get at Grant. The remainder of the herd stood behind her, like a gang of schoolkids egging on the leader to beat up some hapless kid. Grant remembered being that hapless kid a few dozen times in his life. This situation was going to end a lot worse than those had.

Up above him, mud covered most of the dam's top. But daylight beckoned through one Grant-sized gap to his left. He angled in that direction.

The matriarch trumpeted in frustration, as if she was sensing that Grant was getting away. She stepped back, lowered her massive head, and charged the dam. Thousands of kilos of mammoth struck the dam like a pile driver, directly under Grant.

The structure shook like an earthquake had hit. Bark and dirt and sticks rained down all over Grant. Behind him, the mud wall holding back the lake cracked. Water hissed through the fissure and soaked his legs. Grant's foot slipped off its narrow perch.

A glance down revealed that the mammoth had broken one of the larger logs at the dam's base. The cracked ends stuck into the dam exactly where Grant had started his climb. If he'd still been there, he'd have been shish kabobbed.

He found his footing and kept climbing. His stomach scraped rough bark and a stray branch drew blood from his side. The mossy surface of the branches made a tight grip almost impossible.

Below, the mammoth backed up farther than before to take another run at the dam. Grant was still a few meters shy of the opening to the top.

The rest of the herd trumpeted, as if to cheer their champion on. The matriarch lowered her head and charged. Grant climbed as fast as his aching muscles would allow. Daylight called to him from above.

The mammoth struck the dam. Logs boomed as they snapped in two. A shockwave ran through the structure and Grant hugged the tree trunk in front of him to keep from falling.

The dam groaned and wood cracked like rifle shots throughout the structure. Earth crumbled and water sprayed out from the dam's lakeside wall with the roar of a firehose. The stink of algae filled the dam's interior. The narrow blast of water pushed more logs out of place. The timber Grant clung to teetered.

The dam was doomed.

Grant scrambled up the last meters and pulled himself into the daylight. The dam shook as he wobbled to his feet. In the lake, the new rush of current through the growing gap had already started plumes of silt swirling through the water. Logs beneath him shifted and the dam sagged.

The mammoths that had taken up stations on the stream bank were still on duty, but their attention was consumed with the matriarch's attack at the base and the flow of water that now rushed around her legs. The mammoth on the bank up ahead of Grant might kill him, but the collapsing dam surely would. He took a deep breath and ran for the edge of the dam.

Behind him, the crack of snapping logs and the rush of water intensified. The dam beneath his feet shook and shimmied as the wall that held back the lake collapsed. Just as he neared the far side, he caught the attention of the mammoth near the edge. Its eyes narrowed and it trumpeted an angry cry.

Grant's heart beat so hard he was sure it would burst. His lungs burned and sweat poured down the sides of his face. He was rushing to and from his own death at the same time.

A surge of water burst through the base of the dam. Boulders at the foundation deflected a stream to the dam's right side, under the mammoth blocking Grant's escape. The torrent scoured the ground under the creature's feet. The earth shifted and the predatory look on the mammoth's face twisted to one of confusion. It looked down and sidestepped to keep its balance. Then the ground gave way.

As if in slow motion, the mammoth tumbled over into the canyon below the disintegrating dam. It hit the rising water headfirst just to the matriarch's side. The momentum of its massive body broke the animal's neck with a horrific crunch.

Grant ran the last few yards along the top of the collapsing dam. He jumped and landed on solid ground. He turned around in time to see the center of the dam sag and then split apart like two huge doors swinging open. The lake seemed to stay in place of its own volition for a split second, and then the surface collapsed as a dark tidal wave of water surged through the dam's shattered structure.

The matriarch looked up at the wall of water as if only now understanding the function of the pile of logs it had been battering. It raised its trunk to cry out, but there was no time. Tons of water hit the mammoth, drove her down, and swept her away.

The rest of the herd had time to turn from the deluge, but not enough time to escape. The wave crashed into the mammoths and sent them cartwheeling down the canyon. The sentinel on the dam's far side cried out, then lost its footing and toppled in after them.

The accelerating water sheared away the remaining sides of the dam. The lake drained with unbelievable speed and force. Tumbling tree trunks and flailing beavers broke the surface and then vanished as the current propelled it all through the new-found opening.

The wall of murky water went white as it accelerated downslope. A crescendo of collapsing trees echoed across the valley as the water swept entire sections of forest out by its roots.

The monumental force of the inland tidal wave held Grant in awe as it rushed away. He could only imagine the horror of seeing it coming.

CHAPTER THIRTY-ONE

Sgt. Brusilov led the patrol uphill.

He'd made the tactical decision to follow the streambed into the woods. He had almost thirty men with him, and he needed to get deep into the forest quickly. Past floods had scoured a wide bank clear along the narrow stream. With this route he could get a team through the forest faster than if they went single file down one of the trails. His men were making excellent time, proving Brusilov had made the right choice.

Normally, he'd have had a squad ahead of him with some new private walking point for the platoon. But he wasn't advancing against armed Chechen rebels. He was hunting unarmed prey. So Brusilov led the platoon from the front, with two columns of soldiers behind him, one on each side of the creek. When they came across the Americans, he did not want to miss any of the fun.

A hundred meters up, the valley curved to the left and trees obscured what lay ahead. He remembered the bend in the stream from the map. Brusilov checked his watch. They'd be getting to the lake in minutes. Sgt. Petrov had believed that would be the Americans' destination. Brusilov agreed.

A low hum broke the quiet of the forest. The noise grew louder, deeper. Brusilov raised a clenched fist in the air and the platoon stopped. The soldiers took a knee, weapons aimed into the forest.

Brusilov's first thought was of the mammoths. Could they be on the move through the forest? He had enough firepower to take out a tank squadron. He wasn't worried about elephants as long as they didn't sneak up on him.

The noise grew louder. It sounded like the freight trains that used to pass through his village when he was a boy. Not what the mammoths would sound like, but not what anything else out here would sound like either.

Brusilov stroked his rifle's trigger guard with his finger. Over years of service, he'd developed a sixth sense for when a situation was about to head south in a hurry. That sense was sounding an alarm.

Then a mammoth trumpeted from up the valley. On instinct, all the soldiers trained their weapons upstream. Brusilov snapped his rifle to his shoulder and looked down the barrel.

A mammoth came around the bend in the valley, screaming through its upraised trunk. Tusks flashed sharp and polished in the sunlight. Its huge feet splashed in the creek and sent muddy spray all over the low plants in the streambed. Panic filled the creature's eyes.

Brusilov was certain the beast would trample them all.

"Fire! Fire!" he ordered.

A hailstorm of bullets, some of them glowing tracers, converged on the charging mammoth. Rounds peppered the beast, but it did not slow.

The rumbling sound amplified to a deafening roar, so loud it made the air seem thick with the noise. The ground beneath Brusilov's feet vibrated. A wave of fine mist rushed downstream past the mammoth and blasted Brusilov in the face.

Suddenly, a wall of water surged from around the curve ahead. Twenty meters high, it filled the valley. Logs, earth, and mammoth carcasses churned in its black, frothing waters. The water slammed into trees and effortlessly uprooted them. It caught up with the charging mammoth and sucked the beast under like a steam roller.

Gunfire stopped. A cry went up from the Russian soldiers. The men broke for the valley walls.

Brusilov stood his ground and closed his eyes. He remembered a proverb his father used to quote:

One can't have two deaths, but you can't avoid one.

A second later, the wave scoured him and the entire platoon from the face of Mammoth Island.

#

General Vatutin paced the roof of the main building as he smoked an unfiltered cigarette down to nothing. This simple plan he'd made had gone to hell from the start. He blamed Popov, the incompetent fool. He blamed the idiot scientists that had let themselves be overrun by the creatures they had been tasked to master. Most of all, he blamed Destro and the American adventurers who'd come in to steal what was rightfully the property of himself and Mother Russia, in that order.

Even an officer of his rank had to answer for his actions. There would be many questions asked about his "classified mission" when he returned with fewer soldiers than he'd brought into the Arctic Circle. A saber-tooth cat would make the explanation easier; a cat and a woolly mammoth would keep any questions from being asked at all. As soon as Brusilov returned with the Americans' heads on pikes, he'd send his men back out to capture a mammoth.

A muffled boom rolled down the mountain. A cross between thunder and the report of heavy artillery, up from somewhere near the lake. Sgt. Brusilov and his platoon weren't carrying anything that could make that big a noise. He scanned the mountain in that direction and saw nothing.

A trail of mist rose from the distant forest, like a white snake that rose up above the tops of the trees. It made a slow, downhill slither. The mist seemed to be rising off the valley that fed the stream running through the compound.

As the mist drew closer, Vatutin could make out the tops of trees swaying as the mist enveloped them. Some seemed to shudder and fall out of sight. He wondered if a herd of mammoths could make all that happen, then dismissed the idea.

A low rumble filled the air. The volume increased and panic began to swell in Vatutin, as if his subconscious had pieced together the warnings of imminent danger and left his conscious mind a few steps behind.

Tree trunks snapped like the crack of a heavy machine gun. A tower of water appeared in the valley above the compound. The filthy water carried logs and trees and mammoth carcasses atop its frothing surface. It blasted trees into splinters as it barreled downhill toward the compound.

A wide plastic vent tube rose from the roof beside him. Vatutin grabbed it for support. His heart raced and fear overwhelmed all other emotions. The wall had to be almost ten meters high.

In seconds, the surge roared out of the valley and hit the compound. The wave struck the warehouse first. Metal walls crumpled up like tin foil as the water swept the building off its foundation. The height of the wave decreased as the water spread out across the valley floor, but the flow accelerated.

The wave washed over the runway and toward the aircraft. The water's force snapped the landing gear off the planes. Wings dipped into the surging water. Water-borne logs speared one plane's fuselage like warriors' spears. The wave crashed over the second plane's tail and lifted it skyward. Like a breaching whale, it rose to be completely vertical, teetered, then crashed down inverted. The water devoured the plane with the screech of shearing aluminum.

A wave rushed in around the main compound building. The water hit the building and the roof shuddered. Vatutin clenched the vent pipe. A dead mammoth struck the wall and then pinwheeled away. Vatutin dropped to one knee. But his panic diminished as the lowered water level only reached to the windows of the first floor. It shattered glass panes and poured inside, but the structure didn't sway. Water surged around the walls and continued its march down the valley to the sea.

He was going to survive this.

He rose to his feet, placed his hands on his hips and smiled. Few, if any of the men he brought in with him would live through this disaster, but he would be happy to sing the praises of their heroic fight when he returned to Russia. And he would return. He had a satellite phone in the building on a shelf high above the waters. One call and a rescue team would be here for him in no time.

And with him the only survivor, there would be no one else who had to toe the line on the story he'd spin. And what an amazing tale it would be. He'd discovered an American base being built here and his Special Forces had overrun it, only to be wiped out in some kind of Western suicide plan using a lake full of water. All the evidence would be swept up and buried in silt so deep that no one would be able to disprove a word he said.

Somewhere in the building below him, small explosions detonated. The stink of electrical fires belched from the roof vents. The building began to vibrate and a noise like the growl of a bear began. It rose quickly, punctuated by the crunch of twisting metal.

He remembered one of the engineers he'd brought reporting on the geothermal plant. He wasn't listening, too preoccupied with planning his grand reveal for the specimens he'd bring back to Moscow. Something about the generator being unstable, and how if the safeties tripped out, there would be trouble.

The building shook. Vatutin sighed a long string of Russian profanities. He remembered telling Popov that the one at the top can become the one at the bottom in a flash.

#

Grant raised an eyebrow as he looked down from his vantage point by the ruined dam. What had minutes ago been a little creek bed in a valley had been widened and scoured down to bare stone. With the surge passed, the creek had reduced to a tiny trickle of silt. Beneath Grant, a muddy woolly mammoth carcass lay near the top of the bank where it had succumbed to its injuries.

The forest and topography obscured the compound in the valley. He could only imagine the havoc the inland tidal wave had created there.

Suddenly a bright orange flash lit the valley like a solar flare. Grant remembered the warning Deborah had given about how unstable the geothermal reactor had been and what a flood might do to it.

"Oh, hell."

Just as that realization registered, an enormous, glowing bubble hundreds of meters across swelled up from the valley floor. Then a gargantuan geyser rocketed up from the center and burst the bubble. Rock and earth and chunks of concrete sailed a hundred meters into the air. Then came a delayed, muted boom.

Memories of the wind-induced devastation in black-and-white nuclear testing documentaries flashed through Grant's mind. Below him, trees swayed and snapped as a shockwave rolled up the sides of the valley.

Grant dove to the ground, closed his eyes, and covered his head. A hurricane-force wind roared by him, raining dirt and pine boughs everywhere and threatening to suck him off the ground. He hunkered down and prayed.

The shockwave passed. Grant opened his eyes and sat up. A quick check confirmed that all his limbs were still in place.

"Still not dead," he said.

Behind him, the lake had completely emptied. The beaver lodge sat like a hill in the center, or more accurately, a pile of felled trees. The rush of water had scoured the lake bottom out to damp, bare stone. If Destro and the others had stayed by the air vent entrance, they should all be fine.

They might make it out of here alive after all.

If Destro let them.

CHAPTER THIRTY-TWO

Grant went back to the area where he'd come ashore, dragging the sniper's vest behind him.

With the lake drained, the area had reverted to a hillside overlooking a valley, as it had been before the beavers went on their building spree. But where the valley had probably been a lush pine forest, now it was a rocky wasteland. The rush of the water had scoured out any soil and sediment. This moonscape valley would never recover.

Destro, Deborah, and Connor had descended from Beaver Lodge Island and were most of the way across the empty lake. Connor had fashioned a crutch/walking stick out of a branch from the lodge and was making a game attempt at keeping pace. Deborah kept pausing and letting him catch up. Destro just kept walking. The jerk.

Destro crested the lip of the former lake and looked surprised when he saw Grant. "You survived?"

"Sorry to disappoint you."

Deborah and Connor arrived. Connor had one arm draped over Deborah's shoulder as she helped him up the slope. They saw Grant and both broke into smiles.

"Looks like your crazy plan worked after all," Deborah said.

Grant was about to say that it hadn't worked at all, that the grenades were useless smoke and that he'd been millimeters away from being killed by the mammoth matriarch.

"Worked like a charm," he said instead.

"We saw the beavers get swept out with the lake water," Connor said.

"The members of the herd that were around the lake were downstream of the dam," Grant said. "They were all killed in the flood."

"There are probably more mammoths than that," Destro said. "And saber-tooths."

"If they're down in the valley, they won't find their way out," Deborah said. "Looks like pea-soup level fog down there."

She was right. The mist the tumbling waters had produced hadn't dissipated as it should have. Instead, it had intensified into a San Francisco-worthy fog bank.

"What would the after-effect of flooding and blowing up the thermal reactor be?" Grant said.

"The way that one was designed? There's probably a huge crater full of water where the main building used to be."

"And the crater goes down to the magma they used to power the generator?"

"Or at least damn close to it."

"I think the water in that crater's boiling," Grant said. "It's creating steam that's making vapor, and then that hot humid air is hitting cold air and making fog."

"Thanks for the useless weather report," Destro said. "We're going up, not down."

"That hypothesis is far from useless," Grant said.

He dropped the sniper's vest and led the group over to one of the thermal vents that had been hissing at them earlier. It sat silent. He waved a broken pine bough over the opening. The needles didn't flutter.

"That explosion has upset the geothermal balance of this area," Grant said. "Magma's probably shifting, water is creating steam pockets, cooling molten rock is contracting."

A rumble came from downhill in the forest, the sound of stone grinding against stone. The crash of falling trees followed. A plume of dust shot through the fog and into the air.

"What the hell was that?" Connor said.

"A sinkhole," Grant said. "As the pressure and magma supporting the crust disappear, chunks of it will collapse. This whole valley may end up looking like a big Swiss cheese."

"I don't want to get swallowed by one of those," Connor said.

"Odds are we won't," Grant said. "We just need to stay away from any obvious thermal features."

"Like these vents?" Deborah said.

The earth beneath them moaned. Grant turned to run from the defunct vents.

Then the ground collapsed underneath him.

CHAPTER THIRTY-THREE

Grant plummeted down, certain he was about to die somewhere deep in the bowels of the Earth. His scream echoed in the opening sinkhole. Below him, the heat of the planet's molten core promised a painful, sizzling death.

His body jerked to a stop and he hit hard-packed earth face-first. His belt felt like a tourniquet around his stomach. He wiped away dirt from his lips onto his shoulder and then looked down.

The sinkhole had opened up a crater three meters around and at least twenty meters deep. Enough heat rose from the bottom to promise that while the floor wasn't red hot, it was more than hot enough to roast him like a Thanksgiving turkey. The good news was the drop would kill him first.

Grant wondered why he hadn't fallen already. He checked to find that his leather belt had hooked on one of the tree roots protruding from the earth. Now his life depended on how well a long dead cow had taken care of its skin. Splendid.

"Grant, are you okay?" Connor called down.

Grant looked up. Connor, Deborah, and Destro peered down at him from over the sinkhole lip. A tiny cascade of sand flowed off the edge and into Grant's shirt.

"I'm good," Grant said. "My belt caught on one of the tree roots. Throw me down something and pull me out of here."

"Give me your machete," Deborah said to Destro.

Destro seemed to ponder his response, then handed her the blade. Deborah disappeared.

Grant had no clue what they were going to use to save him. The shoreline had been grazed down to the dirt and everything downstream had been washed away.

"Hang on!" Connor said.

Grant waved with both hands. "Cheer on my belt, not me."

Destro looked down, mildly annoyed. "You get yourself into real messes."

Grant wanted to shout that he'd have been sitting on a Hawaiian beach right now if Destro hadn't kidnapped him.

But he was afraid that too much exhaling might make his belt loose and he'd drop to his demise.

The tree root shifted and sent a little avalanche of dirt tumbling down his leg to bounce off his shoe. The quivering root ran up to a stump at the crater's edge. Even if the belt didn't break, the shaking root wasn't making any promises of long-term fidelity.

"Hurry!" Grant said.

Deborah's face returned to the side of the sinkhole. "Here, grab this."

What looked like a thick rope uncurled down the side of the sinkhole. The end slapped to a stop against the ground about a half meter over Grant's head. He reached up with both hands and grabbed it. It felt leathery. Something thick and wet dripped out of the bottom of it and landed on his cheek. He moved his fingers up and down and felt sparse, coarse hairs.

"Oh, hell," he shouted. "This isn't what I think it is, is it?"

"It's a dead mammoth's trunk, you baby," Deborah said. "Shut up and be saved. Everyone pull!"

Grant clamped his hands tight. The trunk moved up and so did he. His belt unhooked from the root and there was no pausing after that. He dug both feet into the side of the sinkhole and pedaled against earth as the three kept pulling.

The trunk stretched in his hands. The cavities within it constricted, and a stream of blood and mammoth snot shot all over his neck and chest. He was too terrified to vomit, but he made a note to set aside time to do that later.

His feet slipped against the soft earth of the sinkhole wall. He feared he was hurting more than helping his chances for getting out of here alive. But each pull from above inched him closer to the sinkhole's edge. As his hands got a half-meter below the edge, Destro and Connor leaned over and each grabbed a wrist with both hands. With one concerted heave, they brought Grant up out of the hole. He landed face-first on the ground with all the finesse of a beached whale. Deborah dropped the end of the trunk and went to one knee.

"When it takes three people to pull you out of a hole," she said in his ear, "might be time to look at cutting down on the all-you-can-eat buffets."

Grant rolled over. "My stomach hanging over my belt kept it from tearing off my pants. If I'd lived your ascetic lifestyle, I'd be dead right now."

"We dodged a bullet with that sinkhole," Connor said.

"That won't be the last one," Grant said as he stood up. "If the steam and the shifting temperatures of the stone continue, the entire structure that supported the valley might collapse."

"More sinkholes, avalanches, and earth tremors," Destro said. "A seismologist's amusement park."

"And our haunted house. But that's only the short-term problem. That network of tunnels and vents fed the warm CO_2-laden air that kept this valley balmy and the plants growing. When those shafts collapse and grow cold, this place is going to revert to the Arctic open-air freezer it was meant to be. The vegetation will die, then so will the mammoths and the saber-tooths."

"And us if we don't get out of here," Connor said.

"Then let's get up to that plateau," Destro said.

"We're guessing where it is with that sketchy map," Connor said.

"But guessing better than if we were without it. We just need a place flat enough for Drew to land. Get climbing."

Destro plucked the sniper's vest from the ground and pulled three magazines from the back pockets. He shoved two in his pocket and replaced his rifle's magazine with the third.

"That's better," Destro said.

"I feel safer already," Grant said. "If you want me to carry that heavy rifle for you just let me know."

"I can manage it. It would be easier if it was one bullet lighter and the group was one wise-ass lighter."

"You'd miss me too much."

"Don't bet money on that," Destro said.

A tremor shook the ground. Somewhere in the forest another sinkhole roared open with the sound of falling stone and snapping trees.

"Follow the edge of the lake." Destro pointed to the mountainside at the other end of the lake. "Our airport is up there."

CHAPTER THIRTY-FOUR

The trek around the lake's shoreline revealed an area that had been denuded by the mammoths and beavers. A twenty-meter-wide swath of dirt and tree stumps ringed the damp downslope that used to be lake bed. A nice place for the plane to land if the stumps hadn't been there to tear out the landing gear. Connor got better at favoring his ankle, and the group made good time across the level, open ground.

At the lake's far side, Grant got an up-close look at their destination. The steep ground rose to what looked like the flat plateau Kai had described. Beyond that, the mountain looked unscalable without a Sherpa team. The top disappeared into clouds, but even the lower reaches beneath the mist were covered in snow. The four began to scale the mountain.

Destro kept checking his watch and shouting for them to hurry up and that timing was going to be tight.

The higher they climbed, the more apparent the valley's changing climate became. Pockets of blue sky appeared as the cover of haze burned away. But despite an increase in sunlight, the temperature kept dropping. It moved from comfortable to cold, especially for Grant in his summer vacation clothing. The good news was that his clothes had dried and it seemed that all the climbing helped keep his body temperature up. At one point, Deborah was nice enough to mention to Grant how body fat was an insulator.

Over an hour later, they reached the plateau. Kai had been wrong. The space was actually a little longer than the valley runway, though it wasn't completely level. No trees grew there, and tall grass ringed the rocky surface. A glacier had advanced downhill so the south side of the plateau rose up to a ten-meter-high wall of frosty ice. It reminded Grant of his old freezer that never defrosted. The end of the ersatz runway sloped down and was already covered in snow, outside the reach of the valley's warm air and tucked into the mountain's shadow.

The group sat down in the high grass just downslope of the plateau. Destro checked his watch and then turned on his radio. It crackled to life.

"Oscar 163," he said into the mic. "This is Destro."

"Destro?" Drew replied. "How can I read you? I'm still too far away."

"I'm up on much higher ground," Destro said. "We have a change of plans. The runway we used before is flooded."

While that was technically true, Grant wondered how forgiving Drew would be later over Destro's sin of omission about the possibility of Russian fighter jets in the area.

"I'm at a plateau on the south end of the valley," Destro said. "There's a glacier on one side. Can't miss it."

"I'll have to take a pass over it to make sure I can land there," Drew said.

"It's fine. Even bigger than the runway in the valley."

"I'll be the judge of that. Oscar 163 out."

"Well, there's some good news for once," Deborah said.

"I may wait to fully exhale until I get home," Grant said.

The ground trembled. Somewhere down in the valley a small avalanche rumbled.

"Do you really think the whole valley could collapse?" Connor said.

"The Yellowstone area is pocked with geothermal locations like this. There's a history of all of them drying up, as well as all of them exploding. Given what we introduced into a balanced system, who knows what could happen."

Off to the east, a plane dropped through a hole in the cloud cover. As it approached, Grant recognized it as the plane that had delivered them. He could not have been happier.

"Oscar 163, we see you," Destro called.

"Roger that," Drew said. "Plateau in sight."

The plane flew down the length of the valley, then made a wide turn to line up with the plateau. It passed over their heads. The roar of the engines was a welcome noise.

"The plateau will work," Drew said. "Swinging around for the approach."

"Thank God," Deborah said. "Time to go home."

Destro stood and waded uphill through the grass a few meters. He turned to face the group and pointed the rifle at them.

"We're not all going home," he said.

Grant jumped up. Destro sent a round into the dirt at Grant's feet. Grant froze.

Deborah rose to her feet with her hands in the air. "I know you have a history with Grant, and he can be annoying."

"Hey there," Grant said.

"But you can't leave him here alone," she finished.

"I'm not," Destro said. "I'm leaving you all here. Did you think I would risk bringing you home with nothing but the promise that you'd be silent about this trip? Hell, Grant here would probably write one of his stupid monster books about it."

"That *would* be a good story," Connor said.

"Destro," Grant said, "you don't need to do this. No one would believe us if we told them what happened, and by the time we get back, all traces of this place will probably be destroyed and buried under meters of snow."

The plane finished its circle of the plateau and lined up to land.

"Even if it was a one-percent chance people would believe you," Destro said, "that's one percent too much. Reference my Survival Rule #3- Minimize your risk."

Behind Destro, the aircraft dropped its landing gear and descended for touchdown.

"So you're just going to leave us here to die?" Grant said.

"Those two? Yes. You? I want the pleasure of shutting your fat mouth for the last time."

Destro aimed his rifle at Grant. Grant looked down the gun's barrel and hoped he wouldn't actually see the bullet coming.

The roar of a saber-tooth tiger ripped through the air. A great cat sprang from the tall grass ten meters from Destro. Its yellow eyes locked on Destro as it charged through the grass, teeth bared for the attack.

Destro whirled around and put the tiger in his sights. He pulled the trigger.

Nothing happened.

The look on his face went from confusion to terror in an instant. He grabbed the charging handle to clear the jam. It didn't move.

The tiger leapt. It hit Destro front-paws-first and drove him to the ground. His rifle flew off to the side. Destro barely started a scream when the tiger delivered a killing bite to his neck.

On the plateau, the plane was about to touch down when the rest of the pride charged it from the grass near the glacier. The closest tiger sprang as it set down on the landing gear.

The plane dipped to that side. The pilot seemed to react to seeing the pride of enormous saber-tooth tigers charging through the grass and over-corrected. He pulled the nose up too hard and too fast. The twin-boom tail struck the ground. It sent up duplicate plumes of rocky dirt from both sides as it knifed through the earth. Then the plane struck something hard and the aircraft pancaked onto the ground. The landing gear collapsed and crushed a tiger under the plane. Propellers hit the dirt at full speed and the blades splintered. Dual fans of shrapnel turned the cockpit area into a colander. The engines stopped with an abrupt shearing sound and the plane buried itself a meter into the ground as it came to a stop.

The plane had killed several saber-tooths on impact. The rest of the pride scattered in all directions. The tiger that had killed Destro crouched over the body and cast a menacing look at Grant and the others. Then it clamped its jaws around Destro's mid-section, picked him up, and ran off.

"Holy crap," Connor said.

"As rescues go," Grant said, "this one sucks."

Deborah went to Destro's rifle and picked it up. She dropped the magazine and looked inside it.

"These bullets are caked in mud," she said. "No wonder it didn't fire after the one chambered round."

Grant remembered how filthy the grenades were when he took them out of the vest. The magazines Destro had taken from the sniper's vest hadn't fared any better.

"I'd thank the mammoth who stomped them into the mud," Grant said. "But she's too dead to take a bow for it."

"Something else that isn't going to happen," Deborah said, "is getting the hell out of here."

CHAPTER THIRTY-FIVE

Grant hated to admit it, but Deborah was right. There was no way they were getting off Mammoth Island.

The cargo plane lay in several pieces on the plateau. The tail boom had broken away on impact and the rudder and horizontal stabilizers sat fifty meters back from the rest of the fuselage. The shattering propellers had ripped both engines out of their cowlings. There hadn't been any sign of life from the plane, and the way the cockpit was shredded, there was no way the pilot or co-pilot survived.

"Maybe someone besides the pilots in that plane knew we were here," Connor said.

"Connor, no one but the pilot even knew there *was* a here," Grant said.

"We'd better see what we can salvage from that plane," Deborah said. She slung the rifle over her shoulder and headed for the wreckage. Grant and Connor followed.

As they got close, the acrid stink of jet fuel filled the air. The fuel tanks had punctured on impact. A new source of anxiety popped up for Grant.

"Hey, can this thing explode?" he asked.

"Not if you don't light a match, create a spark with all these broken wires, or set off a charge of static electricity," Deborah said.

"So, in other words, perfectly safe. Fantastic."

They climbed into the plane through the open rear fuselage. The cargo area was empty. The crew had been here to pick up, not to drop off. The quilted insulation that had covered the interior hung in sheets where the crash had torn it free. The impact of the crash landing had buckled the floor. The door to Destro's luxury cabin hung open. Grant stuck his head in. The giant television was smashed, broken glass littered the carpet, the deluxe leather chairs had been torn from their mounts and lay mangled against the front bulkhead.

At the other side of the cabin, the door to the cockpit had been torn from its hinges, allowing a narrow view restricted to the controls and windshield between the two pilots' seats. Blood splattered the windshield. Grant was sure that was all he needed to see of the cockpit.

"There's not much here," Deborah said. She pointed to a compartment in the ceiling labeled EMERGENCY. "A life raft, as if that would help us out. There's no power to the radio to call for help. This thing is too broken to even be useful as a shelter."

"And it's kind of full of corpses," Grant added.

"What about Destro's radio?" Connor said.

"Destro's tiger didn't bring it back," Grant said.

A shiver raced up Grant's spine, and not because of the proximity of dead bodies. A cold wind blew down off the glacier. He stepped back to the open end of the fuselage. The tips of some of the grasses had turned brown.

"Damn," Grant said.

"What is it?" Connor asked.

"The climate is already shifting. The thermal vents are shutting down and the normal Arctic weather is pushing back in. We'll be wading through snow in a few days. Sooner if a storm blows through."

"We'd better get some wood to make a fire."

"Connor, we're standing in a giant gasoline spill. We'll turn the plateau into a barbeque."

"We'll make a camp downhill, then."

"It will just be a question of starving to death or freezing to death," Deborah said.

A saber-tooth tiger jumped on the horizontal stabilizer of the plane's broken tail fifty meters away. Destro's blood stained its face. It looked at the people in the plane and roared. Fifty meters was way too close to cats that moved as fast as they did.

"That tiger is committed to turning us into a meal before either of those things happen," Grant said.

The remaining members of the pride stepped out of the grass along the plateau. They moved to both sides of the tail boom, three cats flanking the bigger cat on each side like linemen around a quarterback.

"We need to get the hell out of here," Deborah said.

"To where?" Grant said. "We can't outrun the saber-tooths."

"We can out slide them," Deborah said.

She stepped back into the plane and tore a sheet of insulated quilting from the bulkhead and threw it to Connor. She pulled down a second sheet and tossed it to Grant. It felt as dense as the lead vest his dentist used to protect him during x-rays.

"Don't tell me," Grant said. "Becoming saber-tooth matadors is our survival plan."

"Maybe that's your plan," Deborah said, "but not mine."

Deborah reached up and pulled the emergency release for the life raft. A big yellow block of rubber dropped out of the ceiling and hit the floor with a thud. Dust caked the raft.

The tiger on the tail of the plane roared again. This time, the rest of the pride responded in kind. A primal fear squeezed Grant's heart like a vise.

"Get out and get to the nose of the plane," Deborah said. "Now!"

Grant and Connor gathered up their insulation and jumped out of the plane. They dashed around to the nose as the lead tiger leapt down from the tail section onto the stony plateau. Deborah pulled the raft out of the plane and dragged it over to Grant and Connor. She knelt down and gripped a red handle on the raft.

"Cross your fingers," she said.

She pulled the handle. The raft began to hiss and expand. Dirt puffed into the air as sections filled with compressed CO_2. Grant jumped back just before one section flopped open that would have knocked him down. When it finished expanding, the banana-colored raft was about three meters long and half as wide. The bottom had some kind of rigid reinforcement and two small paddles were attached to it.

"Quick," Grant said. "Let's paddle to safety."

"Moron," Deborah said. "We slide. That way."

She pointed to the snowy slope on the far side of the valley's ridge. The steep drop reminded Grant of a black-diamond-level ski trail. He hated snow skiing.

"Are you nuts? We'll be dead halfway down that."

157

"Fine. Stay here and talk the tigers out of eating you."

Grant looked over his shoulder. Between the two sections of the plane, the bloody-faced tiger led the rest of the pride in a low, measured slink in Grant's direction.

"They don't look chatty," Grant said. He threw his blanket into the raft and grabbed the rope handle at his feet. "Let's slide."

Connor tossed his blanket in the raft and grabbed the other side. Deborah picked up the rear and the three ran for the edge of the ridge.

The saber-tooths broke into a sprint. All seven paths angled to converge on the raft.

Grant crossed first into the snowy area. A bitter wind gust cut through Grant's shirt like it wasn't there. His feet sank in the snow and his toes turned to ice. The mad dash turned to a frozen slog. Soon the ground sloped down steeply and the three dropped the raft.

The saber-tooths closed on the group. Unless the big cats harbored an unnatural fear of snow, they would be on the three of them in seconds.

"Get in," Deborah said.

Grant climbed in on his side and Connor on the other. Both dragged in a healthy dose of heavy snow. Grant pulled the paddles from the floor and handed one to Connor. Grant raised his paddle high and dug at the snow like he was paddling a Hawaiian outrigger.

The raft didn't move.

Connor followed his lead on the other side. Still nothing.

The charging tigers were almost at the snowfield's edge.

"Oh, hell," Deborah said. She bent down and raised the rear of the raft. Her muscles strained as she heaved the raft forward. It broke free of the snow and slid free. She kept pushing.

Grant cheered and dug into the snow again with his paddle. The raft moved faster. Connor flailed away on his side as the slope steepened. The scrape of ice against the raft's bottom grew louder as the raft accelerated. Deborah smiled and prepared to heave herself up into the raft. Grant turned to help her in.

The lead saber-tooth hit the edge of the snow. Without pause, it launched itself at the raft. It sailed through the air and landed on Deborah's back. She screamed and lost her grip. The tiger's weight drove her down into the snow. Then it sprang from her back and continued the chase.

The rest of the pride entered the snowfield. The big cats kicked up plumes of white crystal as they converged on their victorious leader. The accelerating raft left the crash scene behind. There was nothing Grant or Connor could do for Deborah.

There also wasn't anything they could do to control the raft. It moved faster down the icy hill than either of them was paddling. It bounced and skidded and threatened to become airborne. Connor dropped his paddle into the raft and hung on to keep from being thrown out.

The raft sent up an explosion of snow each time it smacked the ground. Ice blasted Grant's face and chest into numbness. The raft headed for a set of rocks on the right side of the ravine. Grant stuck his paddle out the rear of the raft to try and steer it away from the rocks. The paddle stuck in the snow and ripped out of Grant's hands.

The raft bounced. In desperation, Grant leaned left. The raft flexed and when it touched down, it careened in that direction. Rocks rushed by on the right with centimeters to spare.

They hit a sun-drenched section that had turned the snow's crust to ice. The raft sped up. The ravine made a banking curve and Grant held his breath as he saw what was ahead.

The slope went almost vertical, hundreds of meters down to the island's base.

Connor screamed. They both ducked and held on for dear life.

The ground fell away. The raft went airborne for a second, and then slammed down hard. Air rushed by and flying ice crystals stung Grant's back like angry bees. The raft bounced again. This time when it landed, something hard punched a dent into the rigid floor. But the raft didn't stop.

Grant tried to look up and see where they were going. The frigid, rushing air sucked the moisture from his eyes. He ducked back down. His whole body shivered uncontrollably.

Then things got worse.

The raft skidded sideways, then backwards, then sideways again. It accelerated into a spin. Memories of vomiting on whirling carnival rides came back to haunt Grant. The rotation quickened as the raft skipped over the snow like a big, yellow pinwheel.

The right side angled down and dug into the snow. That compartment of the raft exploded with a bang. End over end, the raft, the blankets, and the two hapless occupants cartwheeled across the snow. Icy patches sanded the skin on Grant's arms and legs like highway road rash. He lost all orientation for up, down, right or left. It was like being trapped in an icy washing machine.

The whole mess plowed into a snowdrift and stopped.

Grant pulled himself up. His head did a dozen extra spins, and he vomited all over the snow. He put his hands on his knees and spat the hot, acidic remnants from his mouth. He checked the scene through bleary eyes.

They had made it to the base of the mountain. It looked like the edge of the island, based on the snowfield that stretched out in front of him. Connor lay half covered in snow. The raft sat on its side and a quarter deflated. The insulated blankets stuck out of the snow off to his right.

Connor moaned and stirred. Grant went to him and sat him upright.

"Are you okay?" Grant said.

"I think so."

The cold felt like a hundred knives all carving at his skin at once. "Let's make some shelter."

Connor flipped the raft upside down and pounded the snow out of the inside. Grant pulled the blankets out of the snow and shook them clean. Connor leaned the raft against the edge of the snowbank as shelter from the wind and slipped beneath it. Grant crawled under with him, dragging the insulated blankets. He and Connor took a seat and wrapped themselves in the insulation. Grant warmed up to the point where his teeth stopped chattering.

"Did you see what happened to Deborah?" Connor said.

"The tiger got her," Grant said. "At least the attack killed her instantly."

And he meant the sympathy. The woman had been annoying but she didn't deserve to suffer the way Destro had.

"She saved us from the saber-tooths," Connor said.

But for what? Grant thought. *To freeze to death in this Arctic wasteland?*

CHAPTER THIRTY-SIX

"Don't you think it's a waste?" Connor said.

"Are you talking about my books again?"

"No, the destruction of the valley, the eventual loss of those three resurrected species. There's a lot of work, a lot of good science there."

"But work and science for a bad end. I like to think that Nature makes creatures extinct with good cause. A species is either an evolutionary step that improves, or they're an evolutionary dead end. The dead ends get snipped off."

"Maybe early man had hunted these creatures to extinction and Nature had nothing to do with it? You'd bring back dodos if you could."

"Do you think people in loincloths carrying spears hunted those killer mammoths to extinction? Please. Our ancestors, *Homo whatever,* ran from them faster than we did. And besides, early man was just another species at that point in time. We were lucky *we* didn't go extinct."

"This isn't one of your fiction stories," Connor said. "This is a real-life breakthrough."

"And look how much fun it's been."

"But in the right controlled environment—"

"Based on my experiences," Grant said. "Humans and extinct creatures never mix well, in any environment."

They went silent for a while.

"We're going to die here," Connor said.

"I'm afraid that short of a miracle, that may be true."

From above outside came a whining sound. Grant thought it had to be the wind rushing against the raft. But as he listened more closely, he recognized the sound of rotor blades. Grant crawled out from under the raft.

Up the mountain, a bright blue helicopter hovered over the steep drop that nearly destroyed the raft. It was a smaller craft, one of the four-seat models commercial enterprises favored getting to and from remote locations.

"Connor, someone's here!"

Connor stood up and flipped the raft over. He saw the helicopter and gave a shout of joy.

"He still needs to see us," Grant said. "Let's show him this big yellow raft. He can't miss it against the white snow."

They each picked up an end of the raft and began to wave it back and forth in the direction of the helicopter.

The chopper made a circle between them and the glacier, and then dove down into the valley and out of sight.

"Dammit," Connor said.

"Crap," Grant said. "There's no reason for him to look out here on a frozen beach when there's an anomalous biome sitting in the valley."

Just as he was about to give up hope, the helicopter roared out of the valley and directly toward them. They swung the raft back and forth. The helicopter passed over them, then set down in a clear area. It blew up clouds of snow that obscured it. When the crystals settled, it was easy to read the company logo on the helicopter's body. Transworld Union.

Grant sighed as the pilot throttled back the engines.

"I was hoping for the Coast Guard," Connor said. "What's Transworld Union?"

"Just your average friendly global energy conglomerate. But at this point, I think I'll hitch a ride with a group of serial killer clowns if it means we get home."

Grant and Connor ducked down, wrapped the quilts tight, and shuffled over to the helicopter. The deafening scream of the jet turbines made him pull the quilt over his head. The pilot motioned for them to get in the back door. Grant opened the door to reveal two small seats. Connor entered and then Grant. He slammed the door, but it didn't close. He tried again. Still the latch did not catch.

The pilot stuck his head back between the seats. He was all flight helmet and smoked visor to Grant. He passed a headset back to Grant, and Grant put it on. It muffled most of the outside noise.

"Door latches aren't worth a damn in this cold," the pilot said. "This bird's not even certified for passengers because of it."

"We won't tell if you don't," Grant said.

He tried the door again. This time the latch seemed to hold. With the cold sealed out, the heated cabin felt like Heaven. A mass of data screens and equipment took up the space where a co-pilot's seat would have been.

"What the hell are you two doing out here?" the pilot said. He gave Grant a closer look. "And what the hell are you wearing?"

Grant had been so thrilled about their unexpected rescue that he hadn't thought about the story he was going to tell describing this adventure. He opted for a narrow version of the truth.

"We were on a plane out of Yellowknife doing geologic research. It crashed up on the mountain."

"Yeah, that's part of what called me here. I'm working on an oil rig a hundred miles away. Our seismometers recorded an earthquake on this island, and then an automated distress call. I was dispatched to check it out."

"We're glad you happened to find us."

"No accident there. That raft you had sends out that distress signal when you pop it. What the hell are you doing with it down here?"

"We used it to get off the mountain."

"It would have made more sense to stick with the wreck."

"Not the way we were looking at it."

"Any other survivors up there?"

Grant sighed. "I'm afraid not."

"Well sit tight, and I'll have you back to our rig in a half hour."

"Thank you."

Grant strapped on a seatbelt. Connor had heard Grant's half of the conversation and was smiling. Grant shouted at him that they were heading to a Transworld Union oil rig.

"Awesome!" Connor let the blanket fall away from his body, leaned back and closed his eyes.

Grant began to mull the aftermath of all this. Destro and his off-the-books expedition with an off-the-books charter company wasn't going to make any headlines. Neither would the loss of a rogue Russian air force general and a shady oligarch. The Russian government had too tight a control over the media.

Grant didn't know anything about Kai, but he could find out details about Deborah, Ayaan, and Marcus. Their families deserved to know what happened. Whether they'd believe it or not would be a different story. But he guessed it would be better than just having their loved ones vanish without any hope of closure.

Down below, ice sheets seemed to stretch out to infinity. In no time at all, the verdant valley they'd left would look just like the rest of this wasteland.

Connor was sound asleep. He shifted to the left and two thumb drives spilled out of the pocket of his cargo pants. Grant scooped them up off the floor. A roll of papers protruded from Connor's pocket. Grant carefully slid them out.

They were all from the compound. Decryption codes for secret files. Diagrams of the compound layout. A list of files to download, including ones on the *Smilodon* and giant beaver projects.

Connor already knew about the previous monsters Popov had created?

Connor stirred and opened his eyes. He saw Grant with the papers and ripped them out of Grant's hands.

"What's all this?" Grant leaned in to Connor to make himself heard over the rush of the rotor blades. "You took that from the lab? And what's on these flash drives? I thought Ayaan erased all the files?"

"He did." Connor's voice and demeanor were different. Harder. Darker. "Those are his files. I stole them from him just before he tried to defect to the Russians. You're welcome for that, by the way."

"What are you going to do? Sell these to the highest bidder?"

"Turn them over to my employer, Wantami Enterprises. They're worth a fortune."

"I thought you were an out-of-work college drop out?"

"I was until Wantami recruited me. They were one of Popov's investors in this stupid mammoth farm. They had a deal with your buddy Mike Rabon to double-cross Destro. When Destro told them you were going to take Rabon's place, they doubted you'd be able or willing to do the same. So, they hired me to join you. All I had to do was get back to them with my copy of all the research. Well, that plan went to hell, but it's still going to work out in the end."

Grant felt gut-punched. He'd looked after Connor since they both ended up on Destro's plane, worried about him during animal attacks. All the while, Connor had just been playing him.

"You seriously think that this tech is safer in the hands of a Chinese oligarch than a Russian one?" Grant said.

"As long as there's a big payday safe in my hands, I don't care," Connor said. "The worst part of this was having to read all those stupid books you wrote so I could pretend to be a fan. Holy hell, what crap that stuff is."

"You'll never get away with this plan. I'll turn you in as soon as we get to the oil rig."

"Except you aren't getting to the oil rig. Terrible accident with one of those bad door latches. Appears that the door popped open and you plummeted to your death."

Connor turned sideways in his seat and leaned his back against the helicopter door.

"I'll tell everyone what a hero you were," he shouted.

He tucked his feet up to his chest, ready to use them to shove Grant against the lightly latched door and then out into the Arctic. Grant executed a panicked search for anything to hold onto, and found nothing.

Connor kicked.

The small man thought he had enough force to push bulky Grant against the door and out into the cold. But possibly for the first time in his life, Grant's weight worked in his favor. Newtonian physics could not be denied. Connor didn't budge him. But all that force had to go somewhere. Instead of pushing Grant to the right, Connor pushed his own back hard against his door to the left. Hard enough to pop that defective latch. The door swung open.

Connor launched himself out into open space so quickly that surprise didn't register on his face until his butt was sitting on nothing. He windmilled his arms to grab onto something, but his fingers touched nothing but air. He screamed and plummeted down to the ice below.

"What is going on back there?" the pilot shouted through Grant's headset.

Grant fumbled for an answer that made sense without having to resort to the truth.

"The door," Grant said. "Connor fell asleep and must have leaned against it and opened it. I tried to grab him, but I was too late. He never put on a seatbelt."

"Jesus, of all the stupid…You have yours on, right?"

"Hey, I'm still in here."

"Well stay there." The pilot checked the gauges. "Hell, there's no way he survived that fall, anyhow. Damn it, I volunteered to come out here to check out a distress call. I'm not the damn Coast Guard, you know. Now I'll end up in an NTSB investigation. The logbook says this bird can't take passengers, I did it anyway, and one dies. I'll be grounded and lose my license, maybe go to jail."

Grant thought a moment.

"What if no one fell out?" he said.

"What?"

"What if I'm the only survivor you found?"

"Why would you lie about this?"

"Probably because you didn't do anything wrong, and the scumbag who fell out of the door really did. You have my word that I'll stick with the story. I just want to get home."

The pilot looked back into Grant's eyes. He saw Grant was dead serious.

"Then you're the only survivor," the pilot said. "Sorry for your loss."

"That makes one of us," Grant said.

Then Grant had a thought. He'd seen a saber-tooth pound Deborah into the snow, but he hadn't seen one actually kill her. She was pretty tough. Maybe…

"Let's make sure I *am* the only survivor," Grant said. "Head back to where you picked us up and follow our snow trail uphill. I'll show you the crash site."

The pilot scanned his gauges. "I've got fuel for one pass. We stay out longer than that, and someone's going to have to come rescue *us*."

A few minutes later, the helicopter was over the crash site. From the air, it looked even worse with the tail jammed into the ground and the forward section of the plane in pieces. Snow already drifted across the plateau. There were no tracks in the snow, so the shifting weather must have driven the saber-tooths back down the mountain.

"Damn," the pilot said, "you're lucky to still be alive."

Grant hoped that some of that luck had rubbed off on the person who gave his raft the final life-saving push.

"Do you know anyone else survived?" the pilot said.

"I'd hoped so, maybe."

"We got to go back. I am bingo on fuel."

The helicopter leveled out to head back to the rig. Just then, something moved from under the wreckage of the plane's left wing. Deborah crawled out, and began to jump in the air. Snow caked her frozen hair and her skin was as much blue as white.

"There she is!" Grant said. "By the wing."

The chopper banked into a sharp turn and a rapid descent. It landed a few meters from Deborah. She staggered over to the helicopter. Grant reached over and pushed open the door across from him. Deborah climbed in and collapsed into the seat, a shivering mess.

"Got her!" Grant said.

The pilot wasted no time taking off, nose low and skimming the ground.

Grant reached around Deborah, found the seat belt, and strapped her in. She looked up at him and managed a partially frozen smile. Ominous spots of red and black frostbite speckled her cheeks.

"Well, look at you," she shouted.

Grant leaned in closer to her ear to be heard over the rotor noise. "Yeah, still not dead."

"The big cats chased you downhill, so I crawled up and hid inside the engine cowling. The cats couldn't get in."

"You rescued me," Grant said, "and I rescued you. We're even."

"Connor?"

"He didn't make it."

"That's too bad."

"No, it isn't." Grant covered the mic on his headset just in case the pilot could hear him. "Now listen up because by the time we land, we need to have the same story about what just went down on that island."

CHAPTER THIRTY-SEVEN

One Week Later

Grant sat in his office with an array of painkillers in his desk drawer and a mug of hot coffee in front of him. His body had taken a beating on Mammoth Island. His bruises had bruises. His attempt to use a rubber raft as a luge sled had left him with patches of sanded skin on his arms and legs. The final impact at the bottom of the mountain had knocked loose a tooth. The dentist said it would tighten back up, but feeling it wiggle in his mouth had been giving him nightmares.

To top it off, as a parting gift, Connor had either bruised or cracked one of Grant's ribs. The doctor couldn't tell which, but the pain was the same either way, as was the treatment. Letting it heal on its own.

A knock sounded at his door. He called out that it was open.

Karen Castillo, one of the graduate students who worked in his lab for the summer, stepped in.

"Hey, Professor Coleman! How was your trip to Hawaii…?" The last word petered out to nothing as she saw him and her eyes went wide. "OMG, what happened to you?"

"Nothing we're going to talk about. What can I do for you?"

"A huge crate arrived for you. Really huge, like delivered with a forklift huge. Here's the note attached to the bill of lading."

She handed Grant an envelope with his name on it. The return address was from Deborah Becker in Texas. He tore the envelope open.

Professor Coleman,

Thanks for making sure I got out of the Arctic alive. Texas is hot as hell in the summer but I still feel like I have some ice inside me that hasn't melted yet. The frostbite ended up healing better than I'd feared. I wish there was some way to get even for what Destro did, but damned if I can figure out how.

Sadly, Grant had to agree with her. There was no way to hold the deceased Destro to account for anything. The whole story would be unbelievable anyway. And by now, the ruins of the compound and the whole valley around it were probably encased in snow and ice that would never melt.

Inside this crate you'll find the T-rex skull that set this whole nightmare in motion. I hope that you can use it teaching your students, and some good can come out of all this bad.

-Deborah Becker

P.S. Get a gym membership.

Using a black-market fossil, without proper provenance and documentation, violated everything Grant believed about doing proper paleontology. But with the damage done, he might as well accept the donation. It wasn't like there was a more justifiable owner to return it to.

He had tracked down Marcus' family and delivered the sad news and strange story. He'd tried to track down Ayaan's family, but the tech wizard knew exactly how to erase his own trail, and it looked like he'd done just that. Grant didn't even know if Ayaan had been the man's real name.

He had no idea who Connor really had been, and had no motivation to find out. He got the feeling that Connor had been the kind of person with an expertise in burning bridges. He wondered if anyone would notice he was gone.

Later that day, his phone rang. It was Harvey Rindzunner, his literary agent. Grant wasn't in the mood to talk about writing, but Harvey had some literary irons in the fire for him, and he was curious about how hot they were getting.

"Hey, Harvey."

"Grant, my man. How is the trans-Pacific traveler? Good trip to your island paradise?"

"Colder than I expected, but the wildlife was entertaining."

"Hope you came back with inspiration for your next novel."

"You have no idea," Grant said. "How about the projects you're working on for my current novels?"

"Through the roof, things are really happening."

That raised Grant's spirits. "You got the movie deal for *Monsters in the Clouds*?"

"No, that fell through."

"The television pilot for *Curse of the Viper King*?"

"The studio decided to focus more on sitcoms."

"The foreign translation rights for *Forest of Fire*?"

"Tough sell. You kind of pissed off the Chinese government with that one."

Really? Grant thought. *The bastards did try to kill me when I was there.*

"So how are you defining 'really happening' then?" Grant said.

"Glad you asked. You'll be so pumped over this. Private consultant gig with billionaire Parker Rothman as he digs up some..." Harvey paused and keyboard keys tapped in the background. "...itchy thorax?"

"*Ichthyosaur*," Grant corrected. "A giant reptile fish from the Mesozoic era."

"Sure, Mesotastic, right. Anyhow, he's building an eco-friendly resort in the Pacific, wants a consultant to curate a display of the fossils they found during construction. There's talk of a documentary with you as the expert. Really boost your brand recognition."

"I don't know. I don't want to be some ignorant billionaire's private scientist."

"Remember what that movie deal would have been worth?" Harvey said.

"I don't forget numbers like that."

"He's paying double that for two week's work, plus expenses."

That was pay-off-the-mortgage money. But in Grant's experience, none of his side gigs ever seemed to go as planned.

"And," Harvey added, "he owns Sable Palm Studios. They make big budget pictures. Doesn't hurt to have him know who you are."

Perhaps Harvey had lined up a winner for him after all.

"All I'm doing is cataloging fossils and putting them in displays?" Grant said.

"Absolutely. You won't even break a sweat."

"I can break a sweat watching TV."

"Look, Grant," Harvey said in the therapist voice he always adopted for the hard sell, "I can't help you if you don't want to help yourself."

Grant pondered the offer. "Okay, I'll do it."

"Good, because I already signed the contract. Airline tickets are on the way. You leave in August and will be back before school restarts. Talk to you soon."

Harvey disconnected. Grant stared at his phone.

Won't even break a sweat, he thought. Maybe his personal life adventures were making him paranoid, but he already had a feeling that he should have passed on this supposedly simple job.

AFTERWORD

Looks like Grant has scraped through and survived another encounter with creatures that should be extinct, or at least the imagined version of them I created. Let's see how close fact is to fiction.

Woolly mammoths are such an engaging subject. Unlike many dinosaurs, they are so closely related to modern elephants that we can more vividly imagine them walking the Earth. In fact, our earliest ancestors didn't have to imagine them at all. They encountered them and left cave art to prove it.

Real woolly mammoths were about the same size as modern African elephants. Males grew to about eleven feet (over three meters) tall at the shoulders and weighed in at a whopping six tons. Females were slightly smaller. Splendidly adapted to cold weather, they had a two-layer coat of long guard hairs and a short undercoat. Unlike my fictional *Mammuthus homicidus*, that fur did not provide a bulletproof coat. The ears and tail were short to conserve body heat. Mammoths had long, curved tusks and four molars, which were replaced six times during its lifetime. I don't know about you, but I would not turn down having more than two sets of teeth. Mammoths were likely grazers.

Mammoths are believed to have disappeared from most places at the end of the Pleistocene, 10,000 years ago. Evidence suggests that isolated populations survived on St. Paul Island until 5,600 years ago and on Wrangel Island until 4,000 years ago.

One theory is that human beings hunted them to extinction. While a number of people would like to use that theory to make mammoths an anti-hunting poster child, I find it hard to swallow. A small number of humans with stone-tipped spears exterminated six-ton intelligent monsters that could outrun and out-stomp them? Ten thousand years later, far more advanced humans in Africa in far greater numbers using better weapons hadn't wiped out elephants. Pushing elephants to the edge of extinction took gunpowder. With dozens of other species of mammalian megafauna dying out at the same time, it seems much more likely that a global calamity other than the *homo* species was to blame.

Frozen mammoths are still occasionally found in Arctic locations, and have been for centuries. My post-apocalyptic novel *Q Island* is based on what happens when some of the ultra-rich decide that meat is worth eating. The reference in this book to finding a complete baby mammoth in Siberia is to an actual event. The little guy was extracted like an elephant in a block of ice and flown off to be researched.

Woolly mammoth DNA and the African elephant's DNA are 98.55% to 99.40% identical. Can the woolly mammoth be resurrected from the samples we have? The general consensus is no, or at least not yet. Would I be surprised if one day a group of Russian scientists trotted out a mammoth to an extended drum roll? Not in the least. To paraphrase *Jurassic Park*, we tend to do things because we can do them, without thinking if we should do them.

Another one of those species that died out in the great extinction that claimed the mammoths was the *Smilodon* that prowls Mammoth Island. It's probably the best-known saber-toothed cat. Usually called a saber-toothed tiger, it is about as closely related to a modern tiger as a seahorse is to a horse. Saber-tooths likely preferred forest-dwelling prey such as tapirs, deer and woodland bison.

Saber-tooths were smaller than living lions but likely weighed twice as much. These more muscular cats needed to bring down bigger megafauna prey. Seven-inch long canines helped complete that task. *Smilodon* was likely an ambush hunter, like in the story, since it wasn't built to be a runner or a tree climber.

A huge number of saber-tooth bones have been extracted from Los Angeles' LaBrea tar pits. A number of those bones show healed fractures or advanced age. Those findings suggest that injured or older cats might have survived with help from a large pride, so my *Smilodons* hunt Grant and his pals in a group. This is a species we should certainly keep extinct. It's bad enough worrying about mountain lions when I hike near

Topanga Canyon. I'd hate to also have to worry about roaming prides of saber-tooths.

The last creature Grant's diminishing band of explorers encounters are giant beavers. These also used to swim in North American rivers. And they needed rivers, because these things were big.

The species was called *Castoroides* and were much larger than modern beavers. It's believed they could grow up to seven feet long (over two meters) and weigh up to 275 pounds (125 kilos). Today's beavers grow to three feet (one meter) and can weigh as much as 70 pounds (32 kilos). *Castoroides'* tail was longer and possibly was not paddle-shaped as in modern beavers.

As if a larger size wasn't terrifying enough, giant beavers also had scarier teeth. While modern beavers have incisor teeth with smooth enamel, the teeth of the giant beaver were much larger, up to 6 inches (over 15 centimeters) long with a textured enamel surface. Some believe that with a proportionally smaller brain, giant beavers might not have been as mentally quick as today's version. I chalk this unsubstantiated slander up to propaganda from the powerful modern beaver lobby.

I used current beaver behaviors as a basis for the dam building and lodge construction you read about in the book. Beaver engineering is fascinating and intricate. Please go down the rabbit hole of videos showing beavers in lodges and creating dams. You will be amazed at their skills.

In the book, the mammoth graveyard is attributed to asphyxiation in a meadow poisoned by CO_2. This phenomenon actually occurs in nature. The fumes that emanate from volcanoes include carbon dioxide and hydrogen sulfide, which creates that nasty rotten-egg smell. Both are denser than air, so they tend to sink and pool in low, open spaces. Emissions in one location near Mammoth Lake, California came in at 98% carbon dioxide and 0.005% hydrogen sulfide. Carbon dioxide levels of just 10% to 20% can be lethal. At 70% or 80%, you can be dead in a few breaths.

The areas that emit gases can shift as magma rearranges itself within the belly of a volcano, but they are relatively stable.

In the 1990s, large numbers of trees near Horseshoe Lake began to die because of carbon dioxide seepage through the soil. Dead trees eventually covered over 170 acres. If you hike into someplace that has CO2 warning signs posted, pay heed and remember the mammoth graveyard chapter.

Big thanks go out to my faithful beta readers who comb out inconsistencies and find all my garbled syntax. I'm so grateful to Deb DeAlteriis, Donna Fitzpatrick, Belinda Whitney, and Teresa Robeson. Also send up a cheer for the splendid people at Severed Press who make it possible for me to share Grant's misadventures with you. Their covers are the envy of the giant monster industry.

Looks like there is something fishy going on in Grant's future. He has no idea what he's in for. Of course, at this point, neither do I. But I have a bad feeling that he'll be in the thick of something scary. Until then, you can entertain yourself with the Ranger Kathy West series. She and Nathan Toland are NPS rangers battling the supernatural creatures in our American National Park System. In *Claws,* they fight off giant crabs in the Florida Keys. In *Dragons of Kilauea,* they are in Hawaii battling huge reptiles in a volcano that's about to blow. I promise a fun time for all.

Lastly, I am so grateful to all of you for reading these books. Often, I think about people who might be doing a job that's a drag, getting paid at week's end, and then spending a part of that hard-earned cash on something I created. Entertaining you is a responsibility I do not take lightly. Thanks for making the career I love possible.

-Russell James

Check out other great

Dinosaur Thrillers!

Julian Michael Carver

TRIASSIC

After spending many years in artificial hypersleep, a handful of survivors of the exploration vessel Supernova awaken to find their ship torn to shreds. They are unsure of what happened in space or how they crashed into an uncharted planet. Upon exploration of the new world, they soon realize their destination: The Triassic, the first chapter of the Mesozoic Era. A plan is formulated to escape this terrifying landscape plagued with dinosaurs and prehistoric beasts. The survivors soon discover that there may be an even larger threat looming under the trees than just the dinosaurs, threatening to cut their mission short and trap them all forever in the primitive depths of the Triassic.

Hugo Navikov

THE FOUND WORLD

A powerful global cabal wants adventurer Brett Russell to retrieve a superweapon stolen by the scientist who built it. To entice him to travel underneath one of the most dangerous volcanoes on Earth to find the scientist, this shadowy organization will pay him the only thing he cares about: information that will allow him to avenge his family's murder. But before he can get paid, he and his team must enter an underground hellscape of killer plants, giant insects, terrifying dinosaurs, and an army of other predators never previously seen by man. At the end of this journey awaits a revelation that could alter the fate of mankind ... if they can make it back from this horrifying found world.

Check out other great
Dinosaur Thrillers!

Gustavo Bondoni
TEST SITE HORROR

Lieutenant Max Alexeyev is a Russian Special Forces soldier. His job is to protect his country's interests at home and abroad, not to rescue overly ambitious reporters who have bitten off stories too big to chew. But when his unit gets called to a press event at a laboratory that has been invaded by dinosaurs, that's exactly what he finds himself doing. Fighting both prehistoric nightmares and the products of modern genetic experiments in the forests of the Ural Mountains, he battles for his own survival as well as that of alluring journalist Marianne Caruso and her peers.Unbeknownst to him, however, shadowy human forces are at work to ensure that no one spills the secrets of the research being done in the area.Will they live to tell the story of the Test Site Horror?

John Lee Schneider
AGE OF MONSTERS

Once upon a time, Dinosaurs ruled the Earth.But the Mesozoic era – the Age of Reptiles – came to its cataclysmic end sixty-five million years ago.The Age of Monsters begins tonight.And the world of humankind will crumble. Some will call it Judgment. Some will attempt to fight. Others will simply run. Most will just try and survive. But no one will escape.In the mountains. In the oceans. In the cities and towns. Even up in space.Where were YOU when the world ended?

Check out other great

Dinosaur Thrillers!

P.K. Hawkins

THE LOST ISLAND

Scientists Dr. Eccleston and Dr. Lerner have done many routine expeditions for the Skurzon Corporation in the past, helping the company search the ocean for newly available resources freed by melting ice. They're expecting to maybe find oil at the bottom of the Arctic Sea. What they aren't expecting is a lost island that defies all scientific understanding. When something comes out of the sea and destroys their research vessel, the scientists and the rest of the crew are forced into a game of survival against forces no human being has ever seen alive. If they can survive the giant insect swarms, the man-eating plants, and the dinosaurs, they might be able to live to tell the tale. But when each passing moment reveals murderers in their midst, their survival starts to look less and less likely.

William Meikle

THE LAND BELOW

A treasure hunt into the deepest cave system in Europe takes a turn for the worst. Now rather than treasure it is survival that is at the forefront of the spelunkers' thoughts. But their attempt to escape out of the dark deep places is thwarted. Men are not at home in the depths. But there are things that are, pale terrifying things. Huge things. Things red in tooth and claw.

www.ingramcontent.com/pod-product-compliance
Lightning Source LLC
Chambersburg PA
CBHW061232170626
46809CB00007B/2641